THE MURDER OF A STARLET

THE MURDER OF A STARLET

The Mysterious Murder of Dorothy Stratten

BY

JAVIER R. MCNEAL

THE MURDER OF A STARLET

Copywrite @ 2023 by JAVIER R. MCNEAL

All rights reserved

No part of this book be reproduced stored in a retrieval system or transmitted I any form or by any means, electronic mechanical, photocopying recording scanning or otherwise without the prior written permission of the publisher

TABLE OF CONTENT

INTRODUCTION 1

CHAPTER 1 3
  STRAWBERRY SUNDAE SUPREME 3

CHAPTER 2 49
  THE GREAT PLAYBOY HUNT 49

CHAPTER 3 95
  BUNNY PERFECT 95

CHAPTER 4 143
  PLAYMATE OF THE YEAR 143

CHAPTER 5 186
  RISING STAR 186

CHAPTER 6. 229
  LAST DAYS 229

OTHER BOOKS WRITTEN BY THE AUTHOR
.... **285**

THE MURDER OF A STARLET

INTRODUCTION

Dorothy Stratten was a rising star.

She was blonde and beautiful, a shy girl with a big heart who worked at the Dairy Queen until she was plucked from obscurity and put on the cover of Playboy.

From centerfold to movie roles and she was in love on the way to a Hollywood ending. And then it all went terribly wrong.

So, Marilyn Monroe called Hollywood a place where they'll pay you $1000 for a kiss and $0.50 for your soul. Dorothy Stratten would find that out first hand.

Playboy founder Hugh Hefner thought Dorothy was going to be his breakout star. Legendary director Peter Bogdanovich saw her as his muse.

And her small-time hustler boyfriend from home thought Dorothy was his ticket to the big time. But who was Dorothy really?

And who were these three men fought for her heart hard series?

THE MURDER OF A STARLET

CHAPTER 1

STRAWBERRY SUNDAE SUPREME

It's Thursday, August 14th, 1980, 11 pm.

Private Detective Mark Goldstein sits alone in his car, staring at a nondescript 2-story house on a quiet Street in West Los Angeles.

The guy who Lives in the house hired him to tail his wife, she's having an affair.

Passing headlights reflect off the windshield and then fade away.

Goldstein unrolls the window and a curl of cigarette smoke spirals into the night.

He looked at the two cars in front of the house.

They've been parked there since noon.

The woman he's looking for must be in.

But what are they doing inside?

That's the question Goldstein has been asking himself all day.

THE MURDER OF A STARLET

The two roommates got back a few hours ago, and it's been completely quiet since then.

At 11:30 PM, Goldstein decides to do something he rarely does.

Inside the house, Steve Kushner and his roommate, Patty are sprawled out on opposite ends of the couch when they hear the phone ring.

Patty answers, then passes it to Steve.

Steve Kushner here, he said.

Steve doesn't know the caller is sitting in a Car just outside the house.

Kushner, it's Mark Goldstein I need to speak to Paul is he there?

Sorry, I haven't seen him all day, Mark said

He's gotta be in there, I'm looking at his car can you check? Mark asks

Kushner sighs, grabs his beer, and walks downstairs to Paul's bedroom.

He doesn't come down here often.

THE MURDER OF A STARLET

Paul Schneider likes his privacy, and lately, Paul's been particularly Moody.

Kushner feels along the hallway for the light switch and flips it on.

The door is closed he presses his ear to the door, but nothing.

Paul, are you in there? he asked.

There's a guy on the phone who says he needs to talk to you.

It's quiet.

Paul alright, I'm coming in, Kushner said.

When he opens the door and enters, it takes a moment for his eyes to adjust.

When they do, he's not sure what he's looking at.

There's blood everywhere, on the wall, on the floor.

Kushner's eyes opened wide.

There are two dead bodies, both of them nude.

Is that Paul? He asks himself.

THE MURDER OF A STARLET

The face is so mangled he can't tell.

A woman is lying across the corner of the, her head is almost unrecognizable through the gore.

Then he sees the long blonde hair.

Oh God, he turns to come meet Patty, don't don't, don't go in there, Kushner said.

15 minutes later, private sector Mark Goldstein stands in the living room, the phone cradled in the crook of his shoulder while he smokes.

Kushner sits on the couch with his head in his hands.

The other roommate, Patty, is curled up in an armchair, staring at the TV with vacant eyes.

The police are on their way.

Goldstein is now waiting to speak to someone else who needs to know what's happened.

Finally, he hears the man's voice on the other end, he takes a breath.

Mr. Heffner, it's Mark Goldstein, I'm a private detective I've been working for Paul Schneider.

THE MURDER OF A STARLET

Listen, I'm sorry to have to tell you this, Mr. Hefner, I'm sorry it's about one of your playmates Dorothy Stratten.

When he's done speaking, there's a long pause, then the line goes dead.

Less than 12 hours later, what Goldstein tells Hugh Hefner will be all over the news.

"Playboy Magazine's 1980 Playmate of the Year has been found shot to death, killed apparently by her estranged husband, who then killed himself."

What nobody knows yet is why.

1980 was going to be Dorothy Stratten's year.

Hugh Hefner thought it might even be her decade.

She was just 20 years old, the girl next door with a shy smile and whispery voice, who didn't know her beauty.

But to the men in her life, Hugh Hefner, the director Peter Bogdanovich, and the man she married, Paul Schneider.

Dorothy represented the promise of better things.

THE MURDER OF A STARLET

A Playboy centerfold who could become a mainstream movie Star, amuse who could help revive the dying career of the man who killed her she was a ticket to Hollywood and a dream.

But who was Dorothy? and how did her rise to glamour and fame ultimately lead to her death?

Marilyn Monroe called Hollywood a place where they'll pay you $1000 for a kiss and $0.50 for your soul.

Dorothy Stratten would have found that out firsthand.

THE MURDER OF A STARLET

------BACKGROUND------

It's late afternoon January 1978 in Vancouver Canada, a Chilly 41 degrees.

Paul Schneider has one hand on the wheel of his black Dotson 240Z.

With his other he adjusts the rear-view mirror to get a better look at himself.

He wets his fingers and smooths down his mustache.

At 26, he's already been through his share of Hard Knocks but damn, he looks good.

He hits the gas and then turns to his date, just clutching the door relax, Paul says.

Then he turns up the radio and drives faster.

He cruises past pawn shops and convenience stores with busted neon signs.

East Vancouver's rough working-class drug dealers hang out in the doorways of boarded-up stores.

Homeless people push shopping carts covered in TARP to keep out the rain.

THE MURDER OF A STARLET

Paul cranks down the window to let in some air and fingers the Star of David around his neck

It's not just any Star of David, it's studded with diamonds.

Around town, it's earned him a nickname, the Jewish brand.

He wears it proudly, both the name and the necklace.

He turned sharply onto Hastings Street, and a big red Dairy Queen sign came into view.

He turns to the girl and says, I'm in the mood for some ice cream, sure, she says.

Paul pulls the car up to the curb and screeches to a stop.

He steps out and stops to look at himself in the reflection of the driver's side, The window smooths his hair and adjusts his sunglasses.

He's ropey and small and optimistic 5 foot eight.

He wears a long mink Coat and lizard-skin boots that clack on the pavement.

Paul knows how to make an entrance yeah, he's confident.

When he sees the blonde girl behind the counter, he forgets about the girl he's with.

Dorothy Stratten puts her elbows on the counter and flips through a fashion magazine.

She likes the advertisements, fancy people lounging on yachts or stepping out of limousines living carefree lives, they don't have any money worries or little brothers and sisters at home, all alone, or a mom who's too exhausted to make dinner.

When she started working at Dairy Queen at age 14 years old, it was a nice respite from her life.

She's the oldest of three and her mother works all the time, so it's up to her to take care of her brother and sister.

It's just a

part-time job.

But Dorothy loved everything about Dairy Queen at first, the sugary smells of the Chin Chin of the cash register.

But then she turned 15 and 16 and 17, now she's a month away from her 18th birthday and still wearing a little red uniform with her hair and pigtails and an embarrassing requirement of the job.

But at least it's a paycheck and her boss is nice, an ex-biker named Dave.

He watches out for her he's always saying corny things like *you can do whatever you put your mind to.*

Things Dorothy imagines her dad would say.

She wouldn't know since her dad left when she was three.

And her next dad her stepdad, the strongest memory she has of him is when he slapped her in the face and broke her little brother's arm.

Her mother kicked him out after that, and since then it's been just the four of them.

When things are slow at work, Dorothy daydreams about the future, she'll be graduating soon maybe she'll get a job as a secretary in one of those fancy downtown skyscrapers.

She'll click down the hall in her heels with important papers cradled in her arm.

Sit at one of those electric typewriters and be someone her boss can't live without, *I'm sorry he's in a meeting*, she imagines herself saying, *can I take a message?*

Sometimes late at night lying in bed, she imagines she's famous, living in a big house somewhere the sky isn't so grey.

But who's she kidding?

Where would she go?

She's just a girl from East Vancouver who works at the Dairy Queen.

The girl behind the counter at Dairy Queen is tall, maybe 5 foot nine, with blonde pigtails, ski jump nose full breasts pushing against her red and brown uniform.

Paul wonders how a girl like her ended up in a shit crap place like this.

Can I help you? she asks.

At least that's what he thinks she says.

THE MURDER OF A STARLET

Her voice is so soft and whispery, he's not sure.

Schneider takes off his sunglasses to get a better look.

I will have the strawberry sundae supreme, he says.

What is it about her?

No makeup, no jewelry but what a face.

He imagined high cheekbones and hazel eyes.

What's your name? he asks.

She points to the tag on her chest Dorothy, she says quietly.

He realizes that it is because she has no idea how pretty she is, that's her magic.

One strawberry supreme coming right up.

Paul nods towards the booth against the wall

I'll just be over here enjoying the view.

He turns to his date to follow; he can tell from her face she's fuming.

Screw her if she doesn't like his flirting, then she can walk home.

Paul watches Dorothy work behind the counter, watches the way she moves, and how she talks to the customers.

She carries herself like an awkward librarian, quiet, composed like some half girl, half woman, she's got class.

Dorothy comes over with a towering sundae with extra whipped cream and sprinkles.

When he looks back he'll realize this was the moment that changed everything.

When his future came into focus he could see exactly how to get where he was always meant to be.

When Paul gets up to leave, he calls over his shoulder and sees *you around beautiful*.

And he's pretty sure he catches her smile before he walks out the door.

At the end of her shift Dorothy's exhausted, she pulled a double again and still has school work to do.

THE MURDER OF A STARLET

She can't stop thinking about the flashy guy with the sports car who called her beautiful.

No one's ever called her that before.

Her boss Dave walks her to the bus stop like he always does saying he wants to make sure she gets home safe.

Normally he's chatty on their walk, but tonight he's quiet.

When he finally speaks, he says, you should stay away from that guy.

Dorothy looks at him, wide-eyed.

What guy? She asked.

But she knows who Dave's talking about.

Dave gives her one of his looks and says the punk in the fur coat. Trust me, Dorothy, I've seen him around his bad news.

Dorothy laughs, he was just a customer Dave and he was with a girl I've already forgotten.

But she hasn't.

When she goes to bed that night, she thinks about the tower of ice cream she made for him, and how he winked at her when he walked out the door.

Where is he from? She wonders why he can't be from here, he's so different from anyone Dorothy's ever met with his fancy car and glitzy clothes, his life must be so glamorous.

Glamorous is one word for it.

A year before Paul Schneider walks into the Dairy Queen and Dorothy Stratten's life, he's dangling from a hotel window in the dead of winter, staring at the asphalt 30 stories below and praying he doesn't die.

"Beat the shit out of me I don't care just let me up" Schneider begs.

He's trying to crane his neck up, but all he sees is the blowing hair and the mouth full of teeth of the man who's holding his life in his hands.

He should have known better than to get involved with the girlfriend of a drug dealer or burn through $15,000 of the guy's money.

Now he has to think fast, which isn't easy when your heart is pounding out of your chest.

Please, I'll do anything, Schneider yells, his voice hoarse. *I'll pay you back, just give me a couple of days.*

Moments like these force the guy to take stock of his life.

Every mistake Schneider's ever made comes rushing back.

He's 25 the last few years he's been a hustler looking for the next big score.

Maybe he should have been a better son his mom tried harder to make things right with his dad, and if he gets out of this, he promises God or whoever's listening that he'll go straight.

The dealer lets go of one of Schneider's legs, this can't be the way it ends, Schneider said to himself, and then he faints.

When Paul opens his eyes, he's lying on his back on the carpet in that hotel room.

He's alive he feels like crying, he is crying.

The dealer's face looms over him he's so close that Paul can smell the guy's breath, cigarettes, whiskey, and gum.

He tells Paul he's got two days to start it now.

When Paul gets the elevator, he knows one thing for sure.

As soon as he borrows some money and pays the guy back, he needs to get the hell out of Dodge.

Paul Schneider had a lot of bad breaks in his life, starting with his shitty childhood in Vancouver's East End.

His parents weren't much on affection or encouragement when they weren't yelling at each other, they were yelling at the kids.

Paul was the oldest, so he got it the worst.

If he had a block for every time his father told him how worthless he was, or how he'd never amount to anything, he'd be a millionaire by now.

No one was surprised when Paul dropped out of school in 7th grade.

But he needed to do something, so he went to work at his father's leather shop, what a mistake.

His feet swelled, his back ached, and the fights with his father had gotten worse.

When Paul was 21, he quit, *I am better than this place*, he yelled on his way out the door.

His father was pissed but So what? The old man was small time.

Paul was gonna do something big.

Paul started hanging out in Gastown, Vancouver's downtown filled with clubs bars, and strip joints.

He was fascinated by what he saw, pimps dressed in Panama hats and long coats corralling their girls.

They had swagger, confident never let anyone push them around.

Paul was always thing and small, he felt small inside too.

He wanted to feel like them, so he lifted weights to bulk up and never missed a day.

He grew a mustache and sideburns to go with his new look and kept them perfectly groomed.

Pretty soon, girls found him attractive and when Paul felt ready, he started running a couple of girls himself.

He liked the feeling of being in control, he tried to show off at a club but backhanded a girl.

But then the bouncer turned around and punched him in the face and he burst into tears, he doesn't like to think about that.

The gang types who control the underworld think he's a joke.

He's afraid of drugs, scared that will land him in jail.

Paul's scared of a lot, of being laughed at, of missing out, of not getting respect.

Paul thought of himself as an idea man, he was always certain the next big score was just around the corner.

He got into promoting the strip club's wet T-shirt contests, and custom cars.

He was always working an angle.

What he can't figure out is why the big breaks always seem to pass him by or worse, go South.

The hotel fiasco was his wake-up call, never again.

He headed South, landing in Hollywood figured he'd take a shot at breaking into the business.

Maybe could be a producer or a star, but he couldn't get in with the People who matter.

When they met it's like they smelled something bad, so he fell back on doing what he knows best, pimping and promoting, but that's a bust, too.

One of his girls ended up stealing from him and his two car shows flopped, leaving him with a bunch of unhappy investors.

So he crawled back to Vancouver with his tail between his legs.

This time he planned on staying out of trouble sticking with promoting, and forgetting the girls.

But still, he can't let go of the feeling that something's just around the corner, a golden opportunity that will get him out of this Lousy town.

That's when he meets Dorothy, the girl who will change everything.

Dorothy's almost forgotten about the guy in the fur coat when her best friend calls from Dairy Queen.

THE MURDER OF A STARLET

"*Listen, some guy just called asking for you and said he was supposed to go on a date with you, he gave me his number and asked you to call him*".

Dorothy's not sure what to do, so she asks her mother.

Nellie tells her not to call, but she calls anyway.

She recognizes his smooth, confident voice right away.

Hi, beautiful it's your knight in shining armor, he says almost like he's purring.

She feels a little embarrassed, but she's not sure why.

When she doesn't answer, he says, *Mr. Strawberry supreme*, that makes her laugh.

He tells her his name is Paul Schneider, and he says he wants to take her out on a date.

I think we got a real connection, he said.

Did you get that from me making you a Sunday? Dorothy asked.

It was the way you handed it over and the extra whipped cream, Paul relied on.

She knows he's teasing, but she's not quite sure how to respond.

She's had one serious boyfriend in her life and his idea funny was to shove an entire meal in his mouth and then talk so the food came burning out.

So what do you say?

Let's go out I'll pick you up all proper and take you somewhere nice.

She has to admit, she's intrigued, but she's nervous, too. I mean, what would she wear on a date with someone like him? Or they talk about?

She blurts out and said *I'm afraid I can't I'm sick*, Dorothy replies.

And suddenly she does feel sort of sick.

OK, no problem, I'll call you tomorrow, Paul said.

And he does and when she still feigns sick, he calls her again, which is when she finally gets up the courage to say yes.

When Paul pulls up to the curb in front of Dorothy's small house, he's dressed to impress, in a long leather coat with a real mink collar.

THE MURDER OF A STARLET

His lucky Star of David and a gold bracelet with his initials PLS studded in diamonds.

He's got a few cars but he decides to bring the 280Z, girls like the Red leather interior.

He gets out of the car and walks up to the door just as Dorothy opens.

She's got on some dumpy outfit, Gray pants, and a baggy top, but she still looks great.

Her blonde hair shines under the porch light.

Let me just get my coat, she says.

Come say hi to my mom, Nelly, Paul takes a couple of steps in and gives a wave, am Paul, how do you do?

Nellie looks like she's just eaten something bad.

Paul knows he's not the kind of guy mothers approve of, but he doesn't care.

She'll come around, and if she doesn't, then screw her.

Don't worry, I'll take good care of Dorothy, he says with his best shit-eating smile.

Nellie doesn't look so sure.

OK, I'm ready Dorothy says brightly.

Should we go?

He held open the door, and Dorothy sat in.

Dorothy still can't believe she's going on a date with such a classy guy.

When he got out of the car and that fancy coat and his shirt on the button showing that necklace with a diamond-studded star, she almost died.

And here she was in plain Gray pants in a boring black top.

She could almost see the shock on his face.

She's pretty sure she wasn't the girl he expected to see, at least her hair is out of pigtails.

In the car she can't think of a single thing to say.

He has to do all the talking; he asks her what she likes to do on weekends.

But what's she going to say? hang out with her sister, write poetry in her journal, whatever she thinks of sounds so boring, but he doesn't seem to mind.

THE MURDER OF A STARLET

He even touches her hand twice; She can still feel the tingle on her skin.

He tells her he wants to take her to his apartment and Cook for her.

She's not sure what shocks her more that he knows how to cook or that he has his apartment.

Everyone she knows still lives with their parents.

He lives in the West End of town, where the rich people live.

It's like some fancy bachelor pad you see on TV, Burgundy furniture, fur rugs, and so many plants, it looks like an indoor jungle.

There's even a giant skylight and a balcony with a sliding glass door and a huge platform bed.

She thinks this must be how famous people live.

Paul serves dinner on a table with cloth napkins, like it's a restaurant, and pours wine in a real wine glass.

As the spoon Monty, it's sweet and sparkly and goes to her head, which is a relief.

He tells her he's a promoter of expensive car shows and big clubs.

Dorothy's in awe, he seems so big time.

He could probably have anyone, why was he with a waitress from Dairy Queen?

He asks her if she has nice dresses to go out in.

He's nice about it, but he must know she doesn't or why would she be wearing a stupid outfit like this?

After dinner, Paul pulls out a guitar and starts to sing some silly love songs he says he wrote on his own, but the way he sings, looking into her eyes, it all feels so romantic.

So of course they kiss and it feels good.

Paul has a way with words, he tells her he knows exactly how she's feeling because he feels the same way too.

He says their lips were made for each other.

It might sound corny coming from someone else, but the way Paul says it, Dorothy believes him.

Later, she writes in her journal *I'm being sweet, talked by an expert, but I want to hear more.*

Paul knows he has to play Dorothy differently than the others.

She's like a skittish cult say Boo too loudly and she'll run for the hills, so he starts slow.

He waits a week to call before he asks her out again, he's surprised when she tells him she can't.

She just started dating some guy.

Paul has never liked the word NO, he sees it as a challenge.

He convinces her to take a drive with him up to Como, Lake.

At the top, he stops the car and listens to the engine tag.

Then he turns to her takes her chin in his hand and says to Dorothy, we like each other, right? Wasn't our first kiss great?

Dorothy admits that it was, but she feels guilty about the other guy.

Well, then let your heart take you where you want to go forget what's right happiness comes from the heart, not the brain, Paul said and She likes that.

He starts taking her out on dates nice places she's never been to downtown restaurants and waterfront strolls.

He showers her with compliments, telling her how beautiful she is and knockout She can be a model, he says.

He says he buys her gifts, little trinkets, dresses clothes that look good on her.

For her 18th birthday, he gives her a blue Topaz ring, it cost him an arm and a leg, but it was worth it.

She almost cried, she held out her hand and watched it sparkle against the light and said she'd never had anything so nice in her life.

You deserve it, he tells her.

Pretty soon they're spending every weekend together, he gets her into clubs like Oil-Can-Harrys and Gas town discos where people know his name.

He can tell she's impressed.

When she asks him why he dances with other women, he tells her it's business, and says he needs models for his car shows, and she seems to buy it.

One night, Dorothy's friend tags along, she tries to tell Dorothy *Paul shouldn't be dancing with other girls in front of her*, and that she should stand up for herself.

Dorothy confesses all this to Paul and they're back at his apartment alone.

He tells Dorothy she'd be better off without a friend like that, she's just jealous of what they have.

After that night, Dorothy cuts her friend off.

Maybe Paul's right, her friend is just jealous she's seeing an older, more sophisticated man.

Paul's a gentleman, he picks her up from work at the end of her shift, waits in front of his car, and holds open the door.

And he's always bringing her presents, no guy has ever done that before; he even buys her makeup.

He's always telling her how beautiful she is, and compliments like this are new to Dorothy.

At school kids used to make fun of her, she was tall for her age and boys would follow her home and call her names, she looked like a beanpole and had beady eyes like a rat.

One afternoon, one of the boys caught up to her and spit in her face, then he slapped her and pushed her down, but Dorothy refused to cry.

When she entered a new school Centennial High, Dorothy kept her head down and made herself small, in the hall she held her books close to her chest.

She was painfully shy and rarely spoke.

Most of the kids didn't even know who she was.

Later, she would tell an interviewer she was scared to death of people.

When Dorothy turned 16, she started to blossom, her breasts filled out, she grew her blonde hair long, and when the cold wind hit her cheeks, her face glowed.

Pretty soon, she started dating a boy, but she was still shy when they had sex she refused to undress in front of him, instead taking her clothes off under the covers.

When they argued, Dorothy always felt bad, she thought it was her fault and she tried even harder.

She always tried to be nice and do the right thing.

But with Paul, for the first time in her life, she feels like she's following her heart.

It bothers her that her mother Nellie doesn't like him at all.

"She says he's rude, he just walks in and plops down on my couch and puts his feet on my nice coffee table, who does that? Does he even have a job?"

Dorothy tries to tell her about Paul's tough home life, and how he's had to make his way in the world.

Sure, he's made some mistakes, but that was before, he's different now, Dorothy says as she tries to defend Paul.

The truth is she half expects Paul to get tired of her, but he never does.

When they're alone together, Paul shares a softer side, she feels honored that he feels safe enough to share his secrets with her.

He even tells her about an old girlfriend who broke his heart, have you ever been in love, Dorothy? He asked.

She doesn't think she has, it feels like you're walking on air, he says.

The two of you against the world, he tells her when you love someone, you have to be willing to die for each other.

It's early April, and Paul is bouncing around his living room, waving an issue of Playboy magazine in the air.

There's a nationwide search for the magazine's 25th-anniversary playmate, he says.

His younger brother Jeff sits in the corner, reading a comic book.

Dorothy sits on the couch, her legs curled to the side.

Just says what about it?

There's prize money, $25,000,

No reaction.

THE MURDER OF A STARLET

Does he have to spell out everything?

OK, so Marilyn Monroe was in the first issue of Playboy, and look at where she went.

Dorothy's just as beautiful as Marilyn.

Dorothy crosses her arms and goes quiet.

What's the big deal? He asks.

Paul, I'm not one of those girls, she says.

No, baby you got it all wrong Playboy is classy, it's like art, he says.

But people will see it, she says quietly,

Her eyes were well with tears.

Baby, you're thinking too much It'll be fun just to look at this, OK?

He opens up the issue he has in his hand and shakes out the centerfold.

It's a young blonde woman, nude, stretched out on a bed, smiling into the camera.

THE MURDER OF A STARLET

She looks like she was painted in gauze.

See, it's arty, he says.

And you're so much prettier than she is, even when you cry.

That gets a smile.

Imagine what this could do for our future, if you won this thing, what it could do for us.

He can see her start to soften; here it comes he thinks, she's gonna say yes, but instead, she says, will you take me to the graduation dance?

Paul's been sitting in front of Dorothy's house for at least 10 minutes.

Finally, Dorothy runs out, when she opens the door, she squeals **I love my new dress** and kisses him on the cheek.

He knew she looked great in it, white so ruffles and spaghetti straps, Sexy.

He picked it out himself.

Paul wears a Sharkskin suit and tie.

He agreed to take Dorothy to the dance as a favor, but now he's looking forward to it.

He missed all his high school dances since he dropped out in 7th grade.

Now he'll show up with the hottest girl at school on his arm.

He's been practicing his John Travolta dance moves and imagining the look of envy on the faces of the stupid high school boys.

But Paul has one stop he wants them to make before the dance.

He takes her to the studio of Uva Meyer, a German photographer Paul knows.

We're getting our picture taken by a pro, he tells her.

Not all those BS balloons and heart backgrounds.

He figures he'll kill two birds with one stone.

He'll get Dorothy used to the camera, and while he's there, he'll tee up an idea with Meyer he's been rolling around in his head.

THE MURDER OF A STARLET

Paul puts his arms around Dorothy and smiles at the camera.

He knows he looks good, but it's Dorothy who shines.

She throws her head back, clocks ahead, and smiles flirtatiously into Paul's eyes, she's a natural.

When it's over, Paul pulls Meyers and tells him about the Playboy contest.

Shoot my girl, Paul says, *I'll give you 1000 bucks if she's picked a finder's fee, she's lucky to win.*

Dorothy brushes her hair one last time and opens the bathroom door.

It's been a month since Uva Meyer took photos of her at his studio and her graduation dance dress.

Now he's here in Paul's apartment to photograph her without clothes.

She walks into the living room and Paul looks up from the couch and smiles.

You look amazing baby, Paul tells her.

Uva fiddles with his camera, adjusting the lens.

Dorothy's still not entirely sure about this idea, but she trusts Paul.

Where should I go? She asked.

Paul points to the platform bed saying every grade playmate is photographed on a bed.

He fluffs up the pillows, smiles, and says to Dorothy, *you`ve got this baby, imagine it's just me here.*

Dorothy takes off her blouse, but then quickly lifts it to cover her chest, she's not sure how to pose. What should she do with her arms? Where should she look?

Meyer waits patiently and finally says we can try another day if this is too uncomfortable.

Paul turns to Dorothy to watch this, he says.

He does a goofy muscle man pose, and then he does a slow striptease down to his briefs.

Meyer starts snapping a few shots as Paul goes full-on Arnold with his chest flexed and his guns out.

Dorothy laughs She can't help it.

THE MURDER OF A STARLET

He's trying so hard and then she lets her blouse drop.

There she is, Paul says.

Meyer turns the camera her way.

What should I do? She asked.

Paul tells her to pout for the camera, flirt with it, and let your hair drop over your eyes.

Dorothy does what he says, but she feels awkward like she's got 10 arms and 10 legs.

She tries not to cry.

Paul tells Meyer to keep shooting.

When Paul gets the pictures, he's blown away.

Dorothy looks even better on film than she does in person.

But now he's got another problem.

How does he get the photos into the right hands?

There are probably thousands of girls who are sending in photos hoping to get into Playboy magazine.

THE MURDER OF A STARLET

What if some dim-witted secretary accidentally drops Dorothy's photo in the trash?

But Paul has a connection, a photographer he met in a strip club named Ken Honey.

Honey knows the editor of Playboy he's even discovered a few Canadian girls who went on to become playmates.

Now that Paul has photos, he can show Honey that Dorothy's the real deal, fuck Uva Meyer and their agreement.

Paul needs the best.

He gets Honey on the phone and says to him, *it's your lucky day I found a girl and she's a shoe for that playmate contest and there's a $1000 Finder fee in it for you if you shoot the pictures.*

He launches into a sales pitch.

She's got long blonde hair, and legs for days, she's a total girl-next-door package.

Honeys seems interested and asks Paul how old is she.

She is 18, Paul replied,

Honey doesn't sound happy now, *The Legal age is 19 I'll need a consent form from the mother.*

Paul tells him he'll get it.

It's a hot day in August for Vancouver, almost 80 degrees.

Ken Honey is standing in Paul's apartment, squinting at the consent form.

It looks like a mother's signature.

Nelly Hoogstraten and big looping valves, but for all he knows, Paul signed it himself.

He shrugs inside his bag, and Paul smiles.

He offers honey and beer and tells him Dorothy will be here soon.

Good.

Honey's ready to get down to work.

But he hopes Paul doesn't plan on staying, girls are always more comfortable when the boyfriend's not around, but Paul doesn't look like he has plans to go anywhere.

I need you to clear out, Honey says.

Paul doesn't look happy about the idea.

Honey knows his type; the guy always wants to be in charge.

Look, honey says *I'll get better photos without you around.*

Honey knows he's got the upper hand, Schneider needs him.

Paul stares at the photographer for a minute, and then his face breaks into a grand, *Yeah, sure man you're the artist, I've got a car show to set up anyway.*

Then he makes his way to the door as if leaving was his idea all along.

When Dorothy gets to Paul's apartment, it's been completely transformed into a professional studio.

There are reflectors everywhere and a guy moving around the lights and furniture.

A man with a beard and a big Hasselblad camera steps forward and extends his hand, *Miss Dorothy I'm Ken he says,* he looks like somebody's grandfather Dorothy thinks, and she feels reassured.

THE MURDER OF A STARLET

Where's Paul? She asked.

Honey says Paul had to set up one of his car shows.

Besides, we're making art here, right? We need our space.

Dorothy nods I'm ready.

As soon as Honey presses the shutter, Dorothy can tell he is a pro.

He's nice, not creepy at all.

He's serious about getting a good shot.

He tells her where to hold her arms and where to put her hands.

She shows her how to stand to catch the best light.

She's surprised how much easier it is the second time around.

Without Paul here, she doesn't feel as nervous she could just be herself.

It's kind of freeing, in a way.

When it's over, honey hands are a short form he needs to submit with the photos.

THE MURDER OF A STARLET

Dorothy bites on the pen cap as she fills it out.

Name and age are easy, but she has to think when she gets to the line for her father's name and occupation.

She quickly scribbled and wrote, *parents divorced, Father's whereabouts unknown.*

For personality traits, she writes Shy, very sensitive, and romantic.

Career ambitions are a stumper when she graduated in June, she got a job at the telephone company downtown, but it's not the job she imagined it would be.

Finally, she writes I would like to become a star of sorts.

The last question says, what would the Playmate experience mean for you?

Dorothy thinks for a minute and then writes, I hope it will help me gain more confidence in myself.

When it's time to leave, Honey says you did great.

Dorothy smiles, she almost believes him.

THE MURDER OF A STARLET

The day after the shoot all takes Dorothy out for pizza near the harbor to celebrate.

Honey called and told him Dorothy was still a little green, but she was a total natural.

He said out of the hundreds of girls he's photographed over the years, no one came as close to her on a first shoot.

He sent the photos off to the editor that morning.

Paul leaned forward took Dorothy's hand and said to her, *we're gonna go all the way, baby, we're gonna win this thing I feel it and it's just the start and the Sky's the limit for us, think merchandise, movies, your beautiful face on a coffee mug.*

Dorothy doesn't look so sure.

Look he says, I've got an idea Let's make a pact, I've got a few deals, cooking with the car shows and promotions, but I'm gonna manage your career.

Let's split everything, 50/50 down the line.

A lifetime partnership Me and you.

What do you say? He asks

THE MURDER OF A STARLET

Dorothy is quiet.

Paul can't quite read her expression.

Then he sees that smile, a thousand watts bright.

She thrusts out her hand playfully and says let's do it.

Paul raises his glass of wine in the air to Hollywood Baby.

THE MURDER OF A STARLET

CHAPTER 2

The Great Playboy Hunt

It's Friday, August 11th, 1978, and Playboy's 25th anniversary contest is down to the wire and Hef still doesn't have a centerfold.

Inside his office, the Playboy Mansion in Los Angeles, he picks up two 8 by 10 photos from the pile on his desk and holds them up to the light.

Hef`s wearing his usual uniform of black silk pajamas and a pipe Jazz played softly from the ceiling's built-in speakers, it always puts him in the mood.

3000 girls from every state in the US and at least half of Canada have entered the contest.

It's always a risk to put out a public car you never know what you'll get.

But it's also where you can find raw talent, that diamond in the rough.

He glances back and forth between the two photos one's blonde one's rough.

THE MURDER OF A STARLET

He's used to this process.

He rates women by instinct.

It's his favorite part of being Hef, that moment when he sees something no one else does and the expression of confidence and personality that transcends the picture.

Neither of the photos he's looking at have it.

He tosses them aside.

The last few years have been tough for Hef.

First, there were the sensors and the women libbers who wanted to shut them down and then there were the copycat magazines who tried to compete with the penthouse and the hustlers that published raunchier photos and graphic nudity.

Readers ate it up, which ate into Playboy's profits he had to take drastic measures.

A new CEO was brought then there were layoffs.

They had to shut down some of the Playboy clubs.

He won that battle, but there were always more competitors ready to take him down.

THE MURDER OF A STARLET

With this 25th anniversary issue, Hef wants to prove to the world why his magazine is the original and the best.

An illustrated history of Playboy's last quarter century with the promise of excellence for the next 25 years, which is why the centerfold has to be perfect.

A woman in her early 40s with dark blonde hair pokes her head in the door, everyone decent? She asks

Hef laughs, come on in Moe.

Moe is Marilyn Grabowski, Playboy's West Coast editor for the past 14 years.

He calls her his secret weapon.

She has an eye for talent and sees things in photos that other people don't.

It's your lucky day, Moe says and hands him a Manila envelope.

Take a look, she says.

I hope there's magic Pixie dust in there, Hef asks.

THE MURDER OF A STARLET

He pulls out a handful of photos and spreads them out on the desk, who is she? he asks

A complete unknown, she came in from our Stringer in Canada, Dorothy is something, Moe replied.

Hef holds a photo up to the light what a smile.

Hef flips through a few more, some awkward poses she doesn't know where to put her hands but she's got something.

How soon can you get her down here? Hef asks,

How soon do you want her? Moe replied,

Yesterday Hef says I want her here yesterday.

****

Ken Honey scans the crowd at Kerrisdale Arena in Vancouver.

It's Friday afternoon at the World of Wheels, Custom auto show, and the venue is packed with car lovers.

THE MURDER OF A STARLET

It's another one of Paul Schneider's high-concept promotions, psychedelic light shows, disco competition, and a macho man contest.

Honey finds Schneider in front of an airbrushed custom band.

He's staging a photo of Dorothy with a macho man contestant.

She's wearing white shorts and a crop top with matching white boots, holding a giant plastic sword over her head.

Paul stands next to the photographer shouting directions, *raise your left leg baby, OK, now put the sword on his shoulder and say your line.*

Dorothy flashes a smile and now says *I dub thee sirvan.*

Perfect Paul shouts.

When it's done, Honey motions them over and tells them he just got off the phone with Playboy's editor.

They love the photos; he says, they want to fly her in for a test shoot.

Dorothy is ecstatic.

But Honey was surprised to see Paul's face twist into annoyance.

Jesus, they've picked a worse time, I have the light show and the contest on Sunday I can't go this weekend, Paul says.

Honey braces himself as he knows Paul's not going to like the next piece of news.

Hey slow down kid, they're only sending 1 ticket, he tells them, for Dorothy only, Honey added.

Paul's face tightens up.

I need Dorothy to run the cash register, I don't trust anyone else with the money. Schedule it for next weekend and we can both go, he tells Honey.

Honey seen this before with Paul, the guys are control freaks, and he reminds them this is a once-in-a-lifetime chance Playboy calls the shots.

Maybe somebody else can run the register this one time, Honey tells him.

Paul shrugs, what else can he do?

He's not going to shoot himself in the foot.

Honey glances over at Dorothy.

Now it's all up to her.

When Dorothy gets home, her stomach is in knots, she's not sure what to do.

She's never even been out of Vancouver, much less flown on a plane.

She wishes Paul could come, she wants to ask her mother, Nellie, if she should go, but she's out of town, plus, Dorothy's not sure she's ready to tell her.

Nellie would never approve of her posing nude.

So she decides to ask her 16-year-old brother what he thinks she holds back some of the details and tells him it's a modeling opportunity in LA, Paul submitted her photos, but she doesn't say it's for Playboy.

Her brother tells her not to go he hates Paul and doesn't trust him, but Dorothy decides to sleep on it.

The next morning she's made her decision, she's going to L.A.

Now she just has to figure out how to get out of work, she writes a note to her supervisor.

"Dear Miss Bentley, I know this is very short notice, I tried to get a hold of you Saturday. My mother phoned me Friday night, she's coming home early from her holidays and I must meet her at the airport in Los Angeles on Monday. I hope I don't upset things at the office, I will return to work Tuesday at 8:00 a.m. I hope you will understand sincerely Dorothy".

She hates lying, but she can't exactly tell Miss Bentley the truth.

Dorothy drops the letter at the office, then she calls Paul.

Surprisingly, he now seems excited, he even tells her he'll drive her to the airport.

Paul pulls into the loading zone at Terminal 6 at Vancouver's International Airport.

It's early morning, but he can tell it's going to be hot.

He looked over at Dorothy and said to her, *so you ready to knock him dead beautiful?*

THE MURDER OF A STARLET

She looks nervous, I wish you were coming with her, Dorothy said.

Next time, baby you're going to do great.

She's wearing a black jumpsuit he helped her pick out her blonde hair shining in the sun.

He opens the trunk, pulls out her carry-on bag, and wraps his free arm around her waist.

Now listen, he says, L. A is big, but it's easy, you just follow the signs to baggage claim where a guy waits for you.

He tells her, they'll probably take her to the mansion, there might even be a party, there'll be a lot of producers and stars there, people you've seen in the movies you, you gotta play it cool. Don't say too much smile a lot he tells her.

She'll likely meet Hef, he's the one she'll need to impress.

Suck up to him, tell him he's good-looking, laugh at his jokes and if he wants to sleep with you, it's cool, I won't take it personally.

Dorothy looked surprised.

THE MURDER OF A STARLET

She shakes her head and tells him she would never do anything like that.

It's Hollywood, baby, the price of doing business, he says as long as Dorothy comes back to him, it's fine.

He tells her to call him when she gets to LA.

And stop worrying, it's gonna be fine, you're a star, this is the beginning of our dream.

As Dorothy walks through the terminal doors she turns back and gives him a little smile and a wave.

Paul waves back and thinks, I hope she doesn't screw it all up.

****

Dorothy lifts the plastic window shade and looks out over the Pacific; she can't believe she's actually on an airplane.

The sensation of rising or speeding through the clouds is exhilarating.

She fiddles with the ashtray and wraps her feet under the padded footrest.

Her fingers find a round button about the size of ¼, and when she pushes it down her seat clines.

She leans her head back, closes her eyes, and tries to imagine what LA will be like.

Paul says you can walk into a restaurant and see a movie star sitting right there, and everyone pretends they don't notice.

She wonders what Playboy will want her to do.

Will she get to meet Mr. Hefner and will he want to sleep with her?

When Dorothy gets off the plane, she follows the stream of passengers heading toward baggage claim.

LAX buzzes with noise and travelers.

When she exits the terminal, the glare of the sun is blinding, so this is why everyone wears sunglasses Dorothy thinks.

Miss Hogue Stratton?

She turns to see a man in a chauffeur's uniform standing next to a black limousine, he's holding open the back door.

Right this way, he says, taking her suitcase.

First time in a limo? he asks.

Dorothy nods yes.

It's a first class ride she thinks as she hops in.

The interior is dark and it swallows her up, she runs her hands over the leather armrests, they're soft like butter. She can't believe there's a mini-bar with liquor bottles and crystal glasses etched with rabbit heads.

Dorothy watches as they drive past a blur of cream-colored homes with orange tile roofs.

Each has a lawn filled with pink flowering bushes, so different from Vancouver.

The driver tells her the flowers are called Bougainville.

Even the name sounds like paradise, Dorothy thinks.

THE MURDER OF A STARLET

On Sunset Blvd the car drives past music billboards 10 feet high, Donna Summer's face tilted back, singing into a mic, Dolly Parton in a skin-tight jumpsuit.

The limo pulls up to the curb of a 10-story building covered in Windows.

This is it, the driver says.

Dorothy opens the door and peels herself out of the car.

A woman approaches.

You must be Dorothy, she says, thrusting out her hand.

She's slim, with long blonde hair and tinted round sunglasses that flash in the light.

I'm Marilyn Grotowski, it's a mouthful I know you can call me Moe.

Her voice is low and throaty in all business.

Welcome to Playboy follow me.

In the elevator, Moe quickly sizes up Dorothy, she's even prettier than her photos, with golden blonde hair and legs for miles performed AT59, but she's easily 5-11 in her heels.

Moe leads Dorothy to her office and motions to a chair.

When Dorothy is seated, Moe gives her the Playboy spiel.

She tells her thousands of girls have sent photos into the 25th-anniversary contest, and if chosen only a handful to fly in for a test shoot.

Dorothy is one of the lucky ones when they see photos, they'll narrow it down to 16 girls who will get modeling contracts.

Only one will win the contest and appear in the January issue.

Then she gives Dorothy the lineup for the day.

First, a limo will take her to the studio of Playboys, top photographer Mario Casilli.

When she's done, Moe will take her to the mansion to meet Hef.

She'll be staying at a guest house on the property, along with some of the other girls.

THE MURDER OF A STARLET

As Moe Prattles on she notices Dorothy hasn't said a word.

She asks her, your flight was, OK?

It was great, Dorothy replied, but I was nervous it was my first plane ride.

Her voice is hesitant like she's wondering if this is the right answer.

Moe realizes Dorothy may look like a woman, but she's just a girl.

Her voice softens, is this your first time in LA?

Dorothy nods.

Well, your last name is certainly a mouthful, Hoague Stratton, but then again, I can't say much considering mine.

Dorothy laughs.

Are you ready to go to work? Moe asks.

Dorothy tells her she is and flashes a smile.

oh boy, Moe says, Mario's gonna love you.

THE MURDER OF A STARLET

****

Mario Cassilly walks through his studio, flips on the lights, and adjusts the reflector.

He works in a quiet suburb of Altadena, just 10 miles from the hustle of Hollywood.

He doesn't usually work on Sunday, but Moe asked him to come in as a favor.

The 25th-anniversary issue has everyone working overtime.

Mario Cassilly is a master of his craft and a legend of the magazine. In his two dozen years at Playboy, he shot more than 50 centerfolds and dozens of pictorials.

Hef may have redefined the girly mag, but Mario helped give its style and class. He's known as the Master of the Soft-focus lens. He knows just where to place the lights to give women that angelic glow.

It's his job to bring the photos to life and transform a girl with potential into a fantasy girl next door.

But to do that he needs to connect with the model, and help her forget about the camera. That's Mario's superpower with his bushy mustache and friendly face, he resembles a doting uncle more than a Playboy top photographer.

He loves to chat and joke, and when he smiles, which is often his face wrinkles in a million places, sometimes he even sings.

When Dorothy steps out on the set, he can tell she's nervous.

His voice is gentle when he tells her where to put her hands and how to position her body like they have all the time in the world.

Loosen those shoulders up he says, now arch your back turn your head to the left, and look right to the lens, beautiful.

To the eye, it looks awkward and uncomfortable.

But in the viewfinder, Mario sees magic just like that.

At the end session, Mario flips through the test shots.

Dorothy doesn't yet know her best angles and how to work with the camera, but a few of the pictures are extraordinary, some of the best he's ever seen in.

Mario has done his job, will be up to Hef to make the final call.

****

Paul throws himself into his workout he still has a couple of hours to kill before heading to the car show.

He lies down on his back and does some presses as a little bit of weight strains to push it out before his last rap.

Dorothy's plane landed in LA hours ago and he hadn't heard a word, she said she called, how could she forget?

He tried calling Playboy, but he's getting the runaround.

He lets his weights drop down with a crash, a guy in the corner some Arnold wannabe doing squats, shoots him some dirty look.

Fuck him.

He crosses to the payphone, drops them some coins, and punches in a number he now knows by heart.

THE MURDER OF A STARLET

Ken Honey picks up on the first ring.

Paul asks him if he's heard anything about Dorothy.

Honey sigh, *look they got her on a schedule, she'll be home in two days.*

He hangs up before Paul has a chance to say anything else.

Paul calls his house, maybe Dorothy left a message, but there's no answer.

He walks over to the leg press past the dude who gave him the hairy eyeball.

He flips him the bird, then drops down and does 50 push-ups like it's nothing. Just has so much energy he doesn't know what he'll do with it all, 50 more, then maybe he'll try the Playboy Office again.

****

Dorothy leans her head against the rear window of the limo and curls her legs to the side.

It's late afternoon and she is exhausted.

The shoot with Mario took hours.

Moe is on the far side of the back seat, sipping a Pepsi in a rabbit highball glass.

How did it go? She asked.

Dorothy tells her it was fun.

Mario made it easier, she says.

Later, she writes in her diary;

"I was a little shy, standing stark naked in front of a stranger, but after a while, I became more relaxed and got into it.

She's relaxed now, the limo's so cool it feels like riding on top of a plush couch.

She wonders if it would be OK to take a nap, but she's too afraid to ask.

The limo turns off Sunset Blvd and drives through a residential neighborhood.

Sycamore trees form a canopy overhead as the car glides past sprawling estates with huge lawns and bright green grass.

It's like something out of an airbrushed postcard.

THE MURDER OF A STARLET

The limo slows in front of the biggest lawn of them all and an electric wrought iron gate slowly opens to a long, meandering driveway.

Welcome to the Playboy mansion Moe says.

Someone once said the driveway is so long it should have its off-ramp.

Around the last curve, the limo enters a courtyard in the center is a white marble fountain filled with angels spouting water into the air.

Behind it sits the biggest house Dorothy's ever seen in her life, it looks like a Gothic storybook castle.

Dorothy hears animals in the distance motels those are the monkeys, there's an aviary too, and a small zoo.

You can walk the grounds later and see for yourself she says, but first let's get you settled in the guest house, watch out for the Peacocks.

Dorothy follows Moe down a flagstone footpath through a Grove of eucalyptus trees.

They walk between a greenhouse and a tennis court to a 2- story cottage with stone walls and a slate roof.

THE MURDER OF A STARLET

This is the bunkhouse, Moe says, go ahead and freshen up and then I'll take you to the mansion. It's movie night, Hef loves movies.

Hef doesn't just love the movies, his whole life is a movie, and he's the star.

He's had several leading ladies, all beautiful and younger than him, no one knows exactly how many women he slept with.

When asked for a number by a reporter, he said how could I possibly know over 1000 for sure.

At 4:00 PM on Sunday, August 14th, Hef pads down the oak-paneled staircase to the main hall.

Since he bought Playboy Mansion West, it's been one long lavish party for the famous and the beautiful.

And tonight is movie night a more casual affair, a buffet dinner, and then a screening of a new release.

His staff calls up a studio that sends over a print one of the perks of being Hef.

At the cool side buffet, a couple of dozen guests are already filling their plates with steak, lobster, and skewers of BBQ shrimp.

Hef prefers simple Midwestern fare like pot roast and soup.

But celebrities are picky, so he has a 5-star chef on staff 24 hours a day.

He's just one of the reasons these parties are the hottest ticket in town.

When he bought the property in 1971, he told his architects he wanted a place that would be something that nobody else had, a fantasy land, a dreamland just like my philosophy about Playboy magazine, and he got what he wanted.

Hef nods at James Kahn, Jimmy'z, one of the regulars the actor made his name as Sonny Corleone in The Godfather, and just like his character, he's got a weakness for pretty women. So do a lot of Hefs bigshot guests, and the mansion never disappoints.

There aren't many rules here, except that one posted above the doorbell conscribed in Latin which says, *if you don't swing, don't ring.*

Hefs knew how to swing, he once entertained 8 Playboy bunnies in his bedroom.

THE MURDER OF A STARLET

Rumors swirl about people having sex in the dark corners of the pools and from aspirators in the game room.

Most of the rumors are true, but It's not always about sex.

liz Taylor used to stop by for cocktails, and Johnny Carson liked to hit balls on the tennis court.

That's the beauty of life at the mansion, you can make it anything you want it to be.

Dorothy clings to her glass of Pepsi like it's a lifeline.

Moe told her it was movie night at the mansion, but it looked more like a movie premiere.

All the party guests look like they stepped off a set of glamorous women in low-cut mini dresses and see-through blouses, and men in tight slacks and shirts unbuttoned to the middle of their chests.

One man wears only a terrycloth robe.

Moe introduces Dorothy to three girls she can't quite hear their names over the thump of disco music.

All three are playmates who were about to be playmates and all will be staying in the guest house too.

They all have blonde hair and bright white teeth. One hugs Dorothy and whispers in her ear, Isn't this just fabulous? Look, there's Hef.

Dorothy's seen pictures of Hef but she never imagined you'd have such an aura around him or that he'd be wearing pajamas but no one bats an eye.

She watches as he puffs on his pipe and chats with guests.

Moe puts a hand on her arm, let's introduce you to her.

Dorothy's kneel starts to buckle as Hef glides over.

Moe says, Hef, this is Dorothy Hogue Stratton from Vancouver, she just got through shooting with Mario for the contest.

Hef holds out his hand and casually kisses her cheek, nice to meet you, Dorothy, please call me Hef and make yourself at home we're all friends here.

Mr. Hefner is the first famous person Dorothy's ever met.

Later, she'll say she was surprised that he didn't act like a celebrity at all.

He was a human being, he had hands and arms and legs and a face just like everyone else.

As she watches Hef move toward the bar with Moe, she realizes he didn't even put the moves on, he was a perfect gentleman.

****

Moe catches up to Hef at the buffet table, where he's spooning double mashed potatoes onto his plate, grabbing some Hef says. This is my mother's recipe.

Moe tells him It's tempting, but she's got a dinner date.

Then she waits.

Go ahead and ask Hef teases.

Moe takes the bait and asks what he thought about Miss Hogue Stratton.

Heff thinks for a moment.

Well, Hogue Stratton sounds more like a substitute teacher than a playmate, but she's pretty seems poised. Have you seen her test shots?

Not yet, Moe says she's shooting with Mario again tomorrow, we'll know more then,

Hef node is good because Cassilly is the best If he can't bring out the Playmate and her, no one can, the proof is in the pictures, Hef says.

Dorothy is surprised at how relaxed she feels on her second day of shooting with Mario.

Mario has a way of making her feel comfortable, he's the sweetest man in the world.

Her biggest challenge is holding back yawns;

Sunday was exhausting she fell asleep halfway through the movie.

After the shoot, Mario takes Dorothy back to the mansion.

Moe comes out to meet them, let's take a look at the proof, she says.

Dorothy's nervous, she thought she did good, but what does she know?

THE MURDER OF A STARLET

When Moe knocks on her door 20 minutes later, she tells Dorothy she has some good news.

Dorothy has been chosen as one of 16 finalists for the contest and Playboy wants to offer her a modeling contract.

Dorothy's eyes open wide, are you sure? she asks.

Moe laughs we're sure your pictures were great.

She tells Dorothy they'll need her back in two days for more photos.

Moe's not sure how long she'll be here maybe two weeks.

So take care of whatever you need to back home and we'll see you soon, she says.

As Moe walks out the door, she turns ohhh and you'll need to change your name Hogue Stratton isn't sexy, we're thinking Stratton, Dorothy Stratton.

****
*

Paul is worried he's losing control; is not a feeling he likes.

He imagined he'd be by Dorothy's side, meeting Hef and making deals.

Now, Playboys calling the shots, saying they want her back right away without him again.

And he has to hear it from Dorothy?

When she tells him they changed her name, he almost blows.

Those are decisions a manager makes; decisions he should make.

He's already working on a new name, Kristen Shields, and that's done by Dorothy Stratton.

She flies back to LA tomorrow for two weeks of shooting as he watches her, she's spilling over with excitement, talking about some zoo at the mansion and the monkeys and Peacocks.

Who cares about the fucking zoo?

Paul wants details, did she see any movie stars and what was Hef like? Did he put the moves on her?

Dorothy says have barely talked to her just a kiss on the cheek.

No one hit on her at all.

No one? he asks.

Paul's not sure he believes her.

Dorothy stops packing and looks up.

Are you mad? She asks.

I'm just trying to look out for you, Paul says, for us. But I'm not gonna be there with you.

He reminds Dorothy that they're in this together, a package to you.

Don't look so worried, she says, then kisses him.

I'll miss you.

Paul softened and said, so we talk every day, right? And whenever I need you?

Of course, Dorothy says, I promise.

****
***

Paul Schneider flops down on his couch, picks up a copy of Hot Rod, and tosses it aside.

Dorothy's been in LA for a week, and Paul's finding it harder and harder to reach her.

He calls the editor the photography studio, he even calls Honey the photographer in Canada who sent in Dorothy's first pictures.

He calls maybe five times a day, sometimes he catches Dorothy, but a lot of times she's busy shooting.

He worries someone's doing a number on her head.

Today, when Paul calls Cassilly's studio, the receptionist answers.

Put Dorothy on the phone it's important, he says.

The receptionist tells him Dorothy's in the middle of a shoot.

I know she's at a shoot that's why I'm calling your studio, Paul replied.

She puts him on hold, and then a man's voice comes on, *hi kid, what can I do for you?* It's Cassily himself.

Paul shifts his tone, h*ey man, I know you're busy there I'm just checking in, wondering how it's going and how's Dorothy doing?*

Cassilly tells him they're getting some great shots.

How does she like it out there? Paul asks, what you have been up to a lot of parties I bet.

Cassilly says Dorothy seems more excited by the limo that picks her up and takes her home than anything else.

Listen, I gotta get back to work, Cassilly says,

Paul tells Cassilly to have Dorothy call him later, but it's too late Cassilly already hung up.

Paul checks the time she should be down in a couple of hours, then he'll try her again at the mansion.

It's 8:00 AM as Dorothy walks the stone path from the guesthouse to the dining room.

She's been at the Playboy Mansion for almost a week, but it all seems so unreal.

It feels like a vacation in paradise.

She writes in her journal:

THE MURDER OF A STARLET

"I was living a wonderful life in the warm sunshine, being catered to 24 hours a day butler to feed me, maids to clean my room. I could have anything I wanted and more".

She shoots with Playboy photographer Mario Cassilly every day.

Most people think modeling is just getting your hair and makeup done and looking glamorous for the camera, but that's not the way it works.

Creating the fantasy image of the girl next door requires long hours and intense focus, it's all about capturing the perfect pose. An elbow adjustment creates the illusion of fuller breasts, pointed toes lengthen the legs and an arched back looks inviting.

Sometimes, Dorothy's not sure she can arch her back anymore or extend her legs any farther without cramping up, but she never complained.

It helps to play make-believe Dorothy imagines herself as someone else, a character completely different from Dorothy HogueStratton,

When Mario tells her to pout, she pictures Marilyn Monroe's head tilted back, eyes half closed.

When he needs a far away gay she pretends she's Jean Marlow's hand on Chin and Vampy eyes that flirtatiously look past the camera.

Dorothy likes the challenge;

Mario tells her she's got great instincts, and with some training, he says she could be a damn fine actress.

No one's ever told her she could act.

Most nights she gets back to the guesthouse and dives into bed, but the Playboy Mansion never sleeps.

There's always a party, even though the heavy drapes and carpeting in the guest house, Dorothy can hear the beat of disco music and giggles echoing from the grotto.

She doesn't want to seem unfriendly, so some nights she ventures to the mansion she chats with Mr. Hefner and his friends or plays pinball in the game house with the other playmates.

Hefner never hits on her, and she never feels any pressure, but she still feels awkward.

She can't get used to the half-naked girl walking around the property.

She's never sure where to look and there are so many men, older men, famous men, all telling her how beautiful she is.

They ask her if she'd like to take a walk through the grounds, and they look at her chest when they speak.

She isn't sure what to do or even who to talk to.

Sure there are always playmates coming and going but there's also an undercurrent of competition, both for the men and a spot in the magazine.

One night at one of Hef's pajama parties, Dorothy drinks too much and dances too hard.

The next morning, she wakes up with a headache and a guilty conscience.

In her journal, she writes:

"a lot of men were entering my life all of a sudden, and a lot of them wanted me. No one was ever pushy or forceful, but talking can be very powerful, especially to a mixed-up little girl. And I am always getting confused, am always getting lonely".

When Paul calls She's a teary mess, I miss you, she tells him all of these people are nice, but everything just feels so strange.

She begs him to come visit, he flies down that night and they stay at a hotel.

Paul tells her it's going to be fine.

Everybody wants something in Hollywood, he says, don't worry I know how this works and I always know how to take care of you.

****

Paul Schneider is in a hurry and the crush of Vancouver rush hour traffic worries him.

He can't be late Dorothy's finally coming home today and he's thought of the perfect way to impress her.

He's picking her up at the airport in a limo, and not just any limo, this one is a stretch, the biggest he could find.

He lowers the divider and shouts to the driver to pick up the pace.

THE MURDER OF A STARLET

Fifteen minutes later they pull into the loading zone.

Paul tells the driver to keep it running, steps out of the back, and leans against the car with his arms crossed and his best Deniro pose.

He watches arriving passengers spill out of the double doors of the terminal, looking for the familiar blonde.

And then she sees him, she hurries over and flings her arms around his neck.

What's all of this? Dorothy asks.

Star treatment for a star, he says.

Dorothy suddenly turns her head and raises her hand, Mario, shouts over here.

Dorothy has one more shoot before she's done a hometown Victoria, so Playboy sent Mario Cassilly with her.

Paul watches him make his way over.

He has bushy, graying hair and a camera bag slung over his shoulder.

THE MURDER OF A STARLET

When he reaches them, he holds out his hand to Paul, *ah, we finally meet pleasure.*

That's the Mario that Dorothy can't stop talking about?

He looks more like some grandpa than a famous Playboy photographer.

Paul squeezes extra hard when he shakes his hand.

Mario doesn't flinch, *nice ride,* the photographer says.

When Paul speaks, he's smiling, but his eyes are hard, *this is for Dorothy and me, we've got plans tonight.*

He points across the street, 20 yards away, *the cab line is over there,* he says.

Dorothy looks embarrassed, but she'll get over it.

Mario says, *of course,* he kisses Dorothy's cheek. *Try not to stay up too late I need you fresh-faced in the morning.*

Paul winks at him just to show him who's boss.

****

THE MURDER OF A STARLET

It's mid-September 1978 and Hugh Hefner stands in front of a light box at the Playboy offices.

His silk pajamas have been swapped out for a light brown suit.

He is surrounded by Playboy staff, including his editor Moe Grabowski.

They are here to decide the winner of Playboys' 25th anniversary contest and it's down to two girls "Candy loving or Dorothy Stratton, Brunette or a blonde".

Before Dorothy entered the race in the 11th hour Hef was leaning toward candy.

She's a 22-year-old college senior Majoring in public relations.

She has a heart-shaped face, dark eyes, and a charming Oklahoma accent.

Hef looks over her pictures. She wears pink Lacy panties and nothing on top except a white knit shawl.

Hef turns to Moe, how does she look in clothes? a body as formidable as this could be a problem to dress, it's a valid concern a playmate is expected to represent the magazine in public at interviews, appearances and parties.

Moe tells him Candy has great style it won't be a problem.

So what about Dorothy? She asks.

Hef picks up one of her photos, she's got that girl next door look, and I do like blondes.

An assistant points out that Dorothy's got a great story too, discovered at a Dairy Queen and never modeled before.

People eat that up and her smile lights up a room, she's luminescent Moe says.

There's no doubt she's beautiful, but Hef wonders if is she ready.

It's not an easy decision, confident, pretty, and safe, or a stunning beauty who has no experience.

Hef looks at Moe you want me to pick Dorothy, don't you?

The last time I checked, it was your name on the masthead Moe says.

Hef takes a puff of his pipe, he's made his decision.

****

Dorothy's at home when she gets the call.

It's Moe Grabowski, and she gets straight to the point.

Playboy has picked a winner for the 25th Anniversary Playmate.

Dorothy holds her breath.

"Everyone loved your photos, including half, of course, but it's more than just photos. There will be a lot of appearances, speaking to reporters, interviews representing Playboy at events, Hef thinks you're not ready yet".

Dorothy tries to hide her disappointment, who won? She asks.

Candy loves her she's graduating from college this year she's comfortable with the press.

Dorothy says she understands.

Moe continues, *"Hey, but I have some good news too we want to make you the centerfold for the August issue, we'll pay $10,000 for your appearance,"*

She tells Dorothy if she accepts, shooting will take six weeks, so she'll need to move to LA.

She'll be expected to come to the mansion for parties and other appearances.

"You'll still need to find a job but we can help with that," Moe tells her.

Dorothy's so stunned, that she's not sure she can speak.

Finally, she thanks her and then she thanks her two more times.

So what's done? Moe says we'll see you soon.

When Dorothy hangs up, the first call she makes is to Paul.

He tells her to come over it's time to celebrate.

****

While Paul waits for Dorothy, he paces his living room and imagines the future.

THE MURDER OF A STARLET

He's got a million ideas it'll be good to be back in LA.

He'll get some new deals going, bigger deals Miss August, and $10,000 is just the beginning.

He can see Dorothy's name on billboards Dorothy on a life-size poster, and Dorothy in a car showing a playmate who will draw the crowds.

He'll charge for autographs.

Dorothy is a star in the making and he's the one who saw it first, now he just has to seal the deal.

When Dorothy walks in the door, Paul Twirls her around, Miss HogueS, he yells.

Then he blurts it out, let's get married.

Dorothy stops surprised look on her face.

Paul waits for her Yes, maybe some happy tears.

But there are no tears, instead, she looks torn.

Ohh Paul, she says.

It almost sounds like an apology.

No, he says not Ohh Paul how about yes? I'll marry you and let's make our dream happen together.

Dorothy tells him it's not that she doesn't want to marry him, she's just not sure she wants to get married yet.

I'm only 18, Paul everything's happening so fast we have time, Dorothy replied.

But they don't have time.

When Paul meets Hef, he wants him to know that Paul is important, he's not just Dorothy's manager, he's her husband, someone to reckon with.

Don't you love me? he asks.

Of course, she loves him, she says.

Aren't we a partnership? We belong together baby, haven't I always told you that you could be a star?

Dorothy's sighs, as always.

Paul knows exactly what to say.

Maybe she's just being silly.

Paul's always been so supportive, without him, she wouldn't even be going to LA.

OK, she says, let's get engaged.

THE MURDER OF A STARLET

Paul scooped her up in his arms and whoops his rocket ship to the moon was taking off and nothing was going to stop it.

THE MURDER OF A STARLET

CHAPTER 3

BUNNY PERFECT

It's Saturday, October 28th, 1978 and tonight is Hefner's annual Halloween party at the mansion.

One of Playboy's biggest bashes of the year.

He makes his grand entrance and then disappears into a crush of ghouls, witches, and space aliens.

Costumes are required, the sexier, the better.

Hef embraces the sexy Halloween outfit before anyone else.

The entire Great Hall is bathed in eerie blue and green lights and the walls rattle from the beat of a spooky disco tune.

Celebrities mingle with models and producers and Jimmy Cohn as usual with his arm draped around his latest blonde and Olympic gold medalist Bruce Jenner is talking the ear off of Miss March.

Half an hour into the party, Dorothy Stratton arrives even across the crowded dance floor with playmates and models everywhere, she's impossible to miss.

She's a vision in white, tight satin pants, a flowy top, and a wide-brimmed hat.

A butterfly is drawing on her face, it's not much of a costume, but no one cares.

Six weeks ago Hef decided to make Dorothy the August centerfold, now she's a permanent resident of LA, embracing her new life as a playmate in training, which involves daily photo shoots, promotional appearances, and sessions with Playboys PR people.

Hef hasn't seen her more than a few times, but word is she's never late, rarely drinks, and charms everyone she meets.

Hef sees a bright future from this August.

Tonight Dorothy's brought her boyfriend along.

He moved to LA with her and she's eager to make introductions.

But before she can say anything, the guy sticks out his hand.

THE MURDER OF A STARLET

Paul, Paul Schneider, says, great to finally meet, I'm Dorothy's fiancée and her manager.

Hef feels the damp palm gripping his hand too firmly.

He quickly looked Schneider up and down, the guy is dressed like a pimp, with skin-tight bell bottoms that might as well have arrows pointing to his crotch and a silk shirt open to the waist, a jeweled Star of David necklace twinkling on his chest.

This isn't who he pictured Dorothy with and it's not just the outfit that doesn't feel right.

Hef asks Schneider if he's enjoying LA.

Schneider tells him he's busy taking meetings, scouting talent, and managing Dorothy's career.

I've got a lot going on, he winks, like he and Hef are in on some private deal.

A Photographer walks by and requests a quick shot, Hef nods.

Snyder snack his arm around Hefs back and smiles broadly into the lens.

When the photographer's done, Hef leans in and hugs Dorothy, *always a pleasure to see you, my dear.*

But Schneider doesn't take the hint.

Hey Hef, I'd love to run a few ideas by you one of these days, maybe over lunch.

Sure, Hef says.

He turns and makes his way through the crowd.

A few minutes later, Hef spots his security chief waves him over and tells him, *I want you to look into someone,* he says, a guy named Paul Schneider from Vancouver, Canada. I want a full background check.

Hef rarely takes interest in playmates' boyfriends, but Dorothy's different.

And Hef can't shake the feeling that Paul Schneider is no good.

****

THE MURDER OF A STARLET

Dorothy sits in the back of a small theatre trying not to crush the photocopied pages in her hands.

She's nervous.

It's Tuesday night in mid-December 1978, three months since she arrived in LA, and she loves her new acting class.

Paul is slouched in his seat next to her, stifling a yawn.

He's taking the class with her, and tonight the students are performing monologues.

The class was suggested by someone at Playboy, and Dorothy liked the idea.

She knows playmates have a shelf life and she's thinking about her future.

The teacher is Richard Brender and she and Paul looked into a lot of instructors and they liked Brender best.

He has a good Rap, both Terry Garr and Farrah Fawcett were once students.

Brender is intense, but he's warm smiles a lot, and tries to keep everybody at ease, which helps Dorothy because she still feels awkward standing up in front of people.

But she's surprised by how much she likes the process, as Brender calls it, she likes losing herself in the character being someone else.

Tonight everybody is watching the girl on the small stage in the front of the room.

Her name is Molly, she's tall, like Dorothy and blonde.

The two have even struck up a friendship, they practice scenes together some afternoons.

Dorothy's impressed by how easy Molly makes it all look, she's good-natured and cheerful.

Paul even likes her and he doesn't like many people.

Dorothy turns to Paul and whispers *she's good*, he whispers back *she's hot*.

When Molly's done, Brender turns to Dorothy and says to her, Miss Stratton, you're up.

His voice is clear and loud as he draws words out, he always sounds theatrical.

THE MURDER OF A STARLET

Dorothy looks at Paul and says to him *here goes nothing.*

Richard Brender watches Dorothy make her way to the front of the class.

Brender taught hundreds of wannabe actors in his day, but few have what it takes to make it.

And he can see there's something different about Dorothy.

He noticed it the first time she read for him, her voice was breathy and soft and her performance was honest.

He immediately thought of Marilyn Monroe.

A lot of the students who auditioned think acting is just memorizing lines and pretending, not Dorothy there was a sweet vulnerability there like Marilyn.

When Dorothy steps on stage tonight, her voice is tentative.

But there's an authenticity to the way she delivers a line.

When she's finished Brender gives her his notes pretty good, but you have to speak up so they can hear you in the back.

Dorothy thanks him in her wispy, clear voice and she says it louder and gets a laugh from the class, even from Brender.

How about you, Mr. Schneider? Render looks at Paul, he says.

The guy hardly even says anything too bad, The first few times he showed up at the class and Brender got him on stage.

Snyder showed promise he had a raw edge, but then he stopped anticipating and told Brender he wasn't interested in acting, he was just there to keep his eye on Dorothy, plus, he was working on some deals.

Paul Schneider Cruises down Hollywood Blvd in his 240Z.

It's sunset and the sky has a golden orange hue.

People say it's the smog maybe you should bottle it, it even makes this big shit Street look nice.

THE MURDER OF A STARLET

Tourists come here looking for stars, but the closest they get are the names of Hollywood celebrities embedded on the Dirty sidewalks.

The rest of the Boulevard is nothing but shabby X-rated strip clubs, discos broken neon lights, and panhandlers.

Since Paul's arrival in LA, he's been out almost every night cruising the street, scoping out the scene, looking for clubs that are right for promotion.

He's got an idea for a contest, he's calling it the most handsome man in LA.

The contest draws crowds, and then you mark up the booze.

He's thinking about a lookalike competition too, John Travolta, Farrah Fawcett, big celebrities maybe he could talk to Hef.

He probably knows Farrah personally, he can make her an appearance, and now she could even be a judge.

Paul's come a long way since that first trip to LA before he met Dorothy.

Back then, he was still doing car shows and running girls.

But all his deals fell apart.

He was just another nobody in a sea of nobodies.

Not anymore, now he's got connections, he's a guy who gets into the Playboy Mansion with a Direct Line to the man himself.

Paul heads West he's heard about a hot disco on Overland Ave called Chippendales.

They're looking for new ways to promote the club, he's got to sit down with the owner.

Twenty minutes later, he was seated at the bar, he waved over the bartender and said to him *I'm here to see Steve.*

The bartender looks him over, and asks him, are you the Mud wrestling guy, Paul smiles and says to him I'm Paul, a disco consultant and I got an appointment.

The guy walks to the back office and says Steve, there's a dude here to see you.

THE MURDER OF A STARLET

Steve, is Steve Banerjee, an immigrant from the Bengali part of India who talks fast, wears flashy suits and badly wants a piece of the American Dream.

He sold a gas station to buy a crappy old club and turned it into a discotheque.

Since then, he's updated the place five times in five years.

He's obsessed with staying ahead of the curve.

He reads the trades and keeps an eagle eye on his competition, checks out what's trendy, and lately, he's noticed a dip in his receipts.

Disco is on the way out and if he's gonna survive, he needs something fresh.

That's when he got the call, the guy from Canada said he was new in town and had ties to Playboy and Hefner.

Everyone says they know someone in Hollywood but if the Canadian guy is for real it could be helpful.

When Schneider walks into his office and holds out his hand, Ben already recognizes the type.

THE MURDER OF A STARLET

It's the red bell bottoms and diamond rings that give them away, this guy's a hustler, Ben said to himself.

Paul Schneider, he says and looks around, *you've got a classy place here and I've got some ideas that could help fill it up,* Paul said.

He sits down in one of the high-back ornate chairs.

Schneider launches into a list of humdrum ideas, wet T-shirt contests disco competitions.

Ben has heard them all before.

What else have you got? Ben asks.

Snyder sits there, grinning for a beat too long.

Then he started talking double speed and said *I was just at the Playboy Mansion, I've been managing one of the playmates I've got connections, maybe we get some playmates here they judge the contests now and that could be a real draw.*

Ben shrugged and said *sure whatever.*

Ben thought for a while and said, *tell me how you'll make it happen guarantee the House and we'll see.*

Paul stood up and said, *I'll get back to you next week, Do you mind if I take these matches?* Paul asks.

Ben waved his hand and told him to take as many as he wanted.

He thinks he'll probably never see the guy again.

****

Most people think being a playmate means glamorous photo shoots, lucrative appearance deals, and money rolling in.

But the reality is photo shoots are grueling and appearances still don't pay the rent, which means Dorothy needs a job.

The only problem is she can't legally work in the US without being sponsored, but Playboy has a way to help.

If a playmate passes the test, she can make extra money at the Playboy Club.

At its peak, the Playboy Club offered men everything they aspired to attain, exclusive membership, five-star menus, and top-notch entertainment.

But the real stars were the beautiful girls in tight-fitting body suits and low-cut tops with bullet rods, they were called bunnies.

But by the time Dorothy arrives in LA in the late 70s, the club's glamour has faded.

An annual membership key costs $40, which means less exclusivity.

The entertainment feels more like performers on the Borscht Belt circuit, and the food is average fare.

But the bunnies are still beautiful, and now they're the primary draw.

In the third week of November, Dorothy gets a job as a door Bunny.

She's grateful for the money that she had no idea the work would be this hard.

Bunnies arrive at least one hour before their shift to get dressed and do their hair and makeup.

That includes applying 3-inch eyelashes and squeezing into a tightly fitted course in three-inch heels.

Then there's the dress code, the nail Polish, jewelry, and eyeglasses are strictly forbidden.

Cuffs and collars have to be starched and spotless, and the rabbit cufflinks must face each other.

All of this is closely scrutinized by a supervisor, also known as the Bunny mother, there are demerits for makeup, incorrectly applied, scuffed shoes, or runs in stockings.

Chipped nails can lead to docked wages.

There are daily weigh-ins before every shift too, which always makes Dorothy nervous.

She smokes to keep her weight down.

In addition to appearance regulations, each bunny is expected to memorize the 26-page employee handbook or bunny manual.

Additional mandatory training includes learning to perform the Bunny dip, the trademark maneuver playmates used to serve drinks, legs together, back curve, and hips tucked elegantly under, no bending at the waist.

Dorothy is glad she doesn't need to learn the dip.

At 19 she isn't old enough to serve alcohol, which is why they made her a door Bunny.

Tonight, two businessmen are the first to show up, Dorothy smiles at them warmly, like she's meeting a friend, another rule for a Bunny.

Good evening, she says, welcome to the Playboy Club can I see your key?

At the end of her first week, Dorothy falls into bed exhausted at the end of her shift.

But she knows it won't be forever, she's been on a few auditions since she started acting classes.

Maybe one day if she keeps working hard, she'll land a plum role.

****

THE MURDER OF A STARLET

In her short time in Hollywood, Molly Basler has met a lot of girls trying to be actresses, but no one quite like Dorothy Stratton.

Dorothy, so beautiful people turned to stare when they walked down the street.

But Molly can't hate her or be jealous because she's so genuinely sweet.

Since meeting at the acting class, they've become close friends.

So when Molly says she's looking to move, Dorothy asks her to be roommates with her and Paul turns out they need to find a place too.

It's late Friday, December 8th, when she and Dorothy finished lugging a big couch into their new West Side apartment.

I need a glass of wine; Dorothy says as she flops down.

Molly says she wants to bless the apartment first for protection and good luck.

She's from a big religious family, and it's the one thing that keeps her grounded in this crazy town.

They yell for Paul, who reluctantly joins them.

He thinks it's a dumb idea.

Molly isn't sure what to think about Paul.

He can be charming sometimes, but he's also kind of distant and rude.

Still, the place is nice, much nicer than anything she can afford on her own.

Molly recites a quick prayer by the front door as soon as they're done, Paul goes back in the living room and flips on the TV.

The roommate situation starts well enough, Molly and Dorothy are usually busy.

Molly waitresses try to book modeling gigs and auditions.

Dorothy's schedule is even more hectic now that she's got a part-time job at the Bunny Club.

They both got acting classes twice a week.

Molly's surprised that Paul doesn't seem to work or do much of anything.

He mostly sleeps late, and when he does wake up, he keeps the shades drawn and never turns off the TV.

She hears him on the phone, trying to wheel and deal all with saying the same kind of stuff.

He brags about the wet T-shirt contest he put on in Vancouver and how he wants to do one here except wet underwear this time.

Or the most handsome man in LA.

At night, he's gone a lot says he's got meetings with club managers and owners.

The only money he seems to have is whatever Dorothy earns.

Molly saw him go through Dorothy's wallet a few times without even asking her.

But Dorothy doesn't seem to mind.

One day, Molly decides to ask her why she doesn't get mad when Paul goes through her stuff.

She wouldn't put up with it.

But Dorothy defends him saying,

he's not a bad person, but he's stressed right now, he'll get his own thing going soon, she says he's the reason *she got the Playboy centerfold. She would never even be in LA without Paul.*

Molly shrugs, maybe Dorothy's right, and it's not her business as long as he makes Dorothy happy.

****

Paul squeezes his car into a parking space on Overland Ave and shuts off the engine.

He takes a moment to pump himself up.

It's January 1979, a new year, a new vibe, a new Paul, new ideas, and the man he's got a good one.

He's been working it over in his head for a few weeks now he got the idea from Dorothy's Bunny costume.

He has to admit, Hef was a genius when he thought of the Playboy Club Concept, beautiful girls and rabbit ears and sexy outfits and guys who overpay for a drink to stare at their cleavage.

That's what gave Paul the idea.

He remembered a club in Vancouver where he hired male strippers to bring in the ladies.

What if he can class that idea up, hire a few male strippers to entertain, and then bring in a bunch of guys to wait tables?

He called them cigarette lighter men because that will be part of their job, like the girl's cigarettes, ladies like that shed and he'll put them in cuffs and bow ties, just like the bunnies.

He runs the idea by his buddy Max Baer Junior, Max was one of the Stars of the Beverly hillbillies.

He played Jethro, the handsome dumb brother but in real life, Max is shrewd.

He's made a bundle producing low-budget movies and promoting motorcycle and car shows.

It's how he and Paul met.

Paul tells Max about his latest idea, a new kind of bar show, one with male dancers at the end of his pitch there's silence.

Finally, Max says, dancers?

Well, more like strippers, Paul replied.

Max was confused and he asked, is this for like a gay joint or something like that?

No, man, it's for the ladies, trust me, this is a great freaking idea. It'll bring women by the truckload.

But Max still isn't so sure.

Fine, Paul thinks I'll catch it somewhere else.

He calls Steve Banerjee the owner of Chippendales.

Two hours later, he's walking through the door of the club.

Paul lays it out like it's the Golden deal of a lifetime.

The cost of the strippers, a cover charge, the number of shows a night, and how much money they'll make.

Look at the Bunny Clubs he says they're raking in cash;

Banerjee thinks it over for a minute, can't be any worse than his regular midweek low.

OK, he finally says, if you get the guys, we'll split the door I'll give you Wednesdays, let me write something up.

THE MURDER OF A STARLET

Paul stands up and holds out his hand, no need it's a deal.

This is gonna be his year.

****

It's Wednesday night, March 14th, 1979 at Chippendales nightclub, and tonight all Paul Schneider could see wall-to-wall women eagerly awaiting the show, all types and ages from grandmas to coeds.

There isn't an empty sit in the house.

Paul walks from the bar to a table where a reporter is waiting to interview him.

Three weeks into Paul's male stripper promotion has caught on big time.

Tonight women lined up for an hour just to get in.

This club is the hottest thing in LA, so the press wants to write about it and Paul is happy to oblige.

He puts a Harvey wall banger down in front of the reporter.

Drinks on the House he says.

She thanks him, but she doesn't reach for the cocktail She's all business.

Why do you think this idea is taking off? The reporter asks.

Paul smiles loving the spotlight, we're giving them something they want to see and they want to see more and more.

He puts a finger to his lips and points at the stage and says just watch.

The lights go down and it just goes beep pumps through the speakers.

All eyes are on the group of men who dance onto the stage.

The woman starts screaming, and their hoots get louder as the guys begin to take off their clothes.

Under their pants they wear nothing but small black underwear, but don't leave much to the imagination, they gyrate their hips back and forth.

Handsome cigarette men wander through the tables in tight black pants and bow ties and cuffs, just like Paul drew it up.

The male version of Playboy Bunnies.

Paul waves at the club owner, he's got a big grin on his face. Paul flashes him a thumbs up.

Since this thing took off Banerjee's been telling people it was his idea, but it doesn't matter, they're gonna make amends.

****

Dorothy's centerfold spread is 3 months away, but that isn't helping her land any acting gigs, at least not yet.

She has headshots made and drops them off at casting and modeling agencies.

She goes through the trades for auditions and circles anything she thinks she has a shot at.

She gets some modeling work if you can call it that.

Most shoes require her to wear a bikini and a smile, but that's easy now.

Some days she races around Los Angeles on the freeways.

She's taking all sorts of classes, from makeup and hair styling to commercial acting classes and aerobics.

She takes every gig she's offered a JC Penny catalog sheet in the valley, a Catalina sportswear at in Santa Monica.

In between, she reads for casting agencies, everyone seems nice, but no one offers her a real role.

And then there are the gigs Paul lines up mostly car events judging hot guy contests.

He charges people a dollar for her autographed picture.

Dorothy doesn't mind.

She likes her new life and the money's not bad, but it never seems to be enough.

Paul's spending it as fast as she makes it and then tells her they need more.

As soon as she deposits a cheque, it seems like it's gone.

It worries her to support them both.

THE MURDER OF A STARLET

But Paul's money from Chippendale should be coming in soon.

The shows have been a huge success.

She just needs to be patient.

Molly is losing her patience with Paul, the longer their roommates, the more she dislikes him.

When Dorothy's not around, he hits on other girls.

He opens her mail, and when Dorothy's home, he bullies her.

He tells her she's not making enough money.

He monitors her food and tells her she has to watch her weight.

He won't let her wear jeans and forbids her from smoking.

Molly doesn't understand Dorothy could have any guy she wants, why him?

Whenever Paul's gone, it's like the sun comes out in the apartment.

Dorothy transforms into a different person.

She and Molly pull up the shades and open the windows to let air in.

They take trips to the corner market for cookies and chocolate ice cream, and Dorothy doesn't even feel guilty when she sneaks a smoke.

They play little pranks, like yelling at college, students passing by their window then ducking out.

They laugh like teenage girls so hard their stomachs hurt.

When Paul gets back, the shades are drawn again and Dorothy goes dark.

One night, Molly asks her point blank, why did she put up with his crap?

Dorothy hesitates and Mumbles something about owing him.

Paul discovered her without him, she wouldn't even be here.

Molly still doesn't get it to her Paul is a loser.

The High Paul gets from the success of Chippendales doesn't last long.

By early April, the deal had gone sour.

He has a falling out with the club owner.

It's not the first time he didn't get along with the business partner, but it's the first time he got the raw end of the deal.

He makes it a few $100 and then Banergy kicks him to the curb.

He says Chippendales was his idea and there's nothing in writing for Paul to prove otherwise.

Now Banergy is off and running with his concept and Paul's got nothing to show for it.

He's pissed back at square one, sitting in the dark apartment he shares with Dorothy and Molly.

He's starting to bug him more and more.

She's always giving him the stink eye when he digs through Dorothy's wallet or when he tells Dorothy she needs to do something with her hair.

Christ, he's her manager.

Molly should be so lucky, that she can't even get an acting job.

But Paul doesn't lose his cool, he doesn't have to yet, he knows he's still got his ace in the hole he's got, Dorothy.

So maybe Chippendales wasn't meant to be his big score.

It means he can concentrate more on Dorothy now.

There are so many marketing possibilities, poster perfume, a book about how she came from nothing.

Hell, she could start her TV movie.

Playboy told her she might even be Playmate of the Year. That's the Playboy Lottery, 200 grands in cash prizes.

She'll be famous and they'll be rich and he'll be by her side for everything, her producer and manager.

But he wants to guarantee he's not gonna make the same mistake he did with Banerjee and Chippendales.

He needs to have something binding, like a marriage license.

They've been engaged for almost 8 months.

THE MURDER OF A STARLET

He's been trying to get Dorothy to set a date, but she's always putting him off.

Paul is done waiting.

Dorothy has a promotional appearance for Playboy in Las Vegas in June.

He circles the date.

They'll get married in Vegas, he'll make sure of it.

****

It's early morning in late April and Playboy photo editor Moe Grabowski is sweating to the beat of a disco song in aerobics class.

The instructor is a little guy named Richard Simmons who jumps around the studio like a madman.

He's got wild curly hair, a high-pitched voice, and an infant smile.

Dorothy takes the class with Moe and usually laughs her way through it, but this morning she looks tired like her head is somewhere else.

It's part of most jobs to get to know all of the playmates, but she's got a soft spot for Dorothy.

She feels like she needs to look out for her and after eight months of working together, the two have struck up a genuine friendship.

Moe takes her to lunch and they talk on the phone regularly.

When the class is over, Moe asks her what's wrong.

I can tell you're distracted, Moe says.

Dorothy admits she's got a lot on her mind.

Paul wants to get married, she says.

Moe sighs.

She's met Paul several times, it didn't take a rocket scientist to know he was bad news.

Moe's been on the receiving end of his calls when he was tracking Dorothy down.

What do you think? Moe asked.

Dorothy looks away and said I owe it to him, she says *'I was in nobody when he found me"*. Moe shakes her head, and says to her, Honey, you were never a nobody, you just thought you were. Whatever you become will be because of who you are not because of someone else.

Moe reminds her she's got a big year coming up when her issue comes out, doors will open.

Don't spoil it, don't do something you may regret later. Live with him if you want to, If you feel you owe it to him, but don't get married.

Moe has no idea if Dorothy is listening, she hopes she is because she means every word marrying Paul would be a huge mistake.

It's late when Dorothy comes home after finishing a shift at the club.

Paul's been waiting up for her.

He starts with a casual question.

Hey, babe, I've got a great idea, you know that Playboy promotion thing you have coming up in Vegas?

He rubbed your neck and said I think we should get hitched in Vegas.

He feels Dorothy stiffen.

I don't know, she says.

It'll just be me and you, come on.

It'll be a hoot. Frank Sinatra got married in Vegas.

But that's like a month away, she says let's think about it.

Paul's voice takes on a note of irritation, this is what we talked about, the partnership all the way.

Then he decides to play hardball.

If we don't get married in Vegas, I'll leave you. Then what will happen to you?

He sees the fear on her face, softens his tone, and then adds, this is what love is we belong to each other.

****

Hef can't believe what Dorothy is asking him to do.

Normally he loves saying yes to his girls anything they want and most of them ask him for a lot of expensive champagne, exotic pets, luxury trips, and jewellery.

THE MURDER OF A STARLET

They get a taste of the Hollywood lifestyle and suddenly they want, want, want.

But not Dorothy until now.

She tells him she's getting married to Paul on June 1st and she'd like him to walk her down the aisle.

Hef is touched, but he can't give her the answer she wants.

Paul is a loser an operator who's using Dorothy, he was surprised his security people couldn't find anything criminal in his background when they called the Vancouver PD.

There wasn't a single arrest or report in their database.

Hef figures the guy just hasn't been caught.

He's a Wheeler dealer through and through.

He takes a deep breath, I'm flattered, Dorothy, he finally says, but my answer is no I'm sorry.

Why Hef? She asks, not able to hide her disappointment.

He chooses his next words carefully, I'm opposed to the marriage, he says. Paul is a hustler, he's a pimp.

Dorothy is quiet, then she laughs and says, Ohh gosh, he's not mad, he's just he was just dressed that way at the Halloween party.

She says it like she's clearing up a misunderstanding.

But has made his decision and urges her to reconsider.

Dorothy drops her eyes and shakes her head.

She's marrying Paul.

****

Dorothy never imagined her wedding would be in a nondescript building with a neon sign out front on the Vegas Strip.

But for better or worse, for richer or for poorer, here she is at the Silver Bell wedding Chapel.

Is June 1st, 1979 on a hot, Dry Nevada Day.

She and Paul arrive in a white stretch limo. Paul paid extra for it, he's going big on everything, even sprung for the $65 deluxe wedding package, which includes a corsage and wedding photos.

He even chose the venue and scheduled it around her Playboy appearances.

Paul's wearing a tuxedo it's Light brown with wide lapels, a white shirt, and dark brown striping on the pants.

Dorothy went with a simple white dress, she picked it because it was practical and she knew she could wear it again.

We look good, Paul whispers to her as he has just his tie and squeezes Dorothy's hand.

Lots of famous people have married here Paul like Burt Bacharach and Angie Dickinson. One day they'll be talking about us, too.

The only other person attending is a guy Paul knows who's going to act as best man.

One of the Chapel employees is Dorothy's bridesmaid.

She feels a pang of guilt, she hasn't even told her.

Paul picks the corsage from a display cooler and then pins it on her.

There's no one to give her away, so Dorothy walks herself down the aisle.

The vows take all of five minutes, then rings are exchanged and Paul bends Dorothy back for a dramatic kiss.

She laughs as Paul dips her and they kiss again.

The employees smile and congratulate them.

It's done, she's married.

Later that night, when she records the day in her diary, she only writes down two words in all caps *"Wedding day"*.

She can't think of anything else to say.

****

Three days later, Dorothy and Paul have a wedding reception at the home of Max Baer junior, an actor, slash producer, and friend of Paul's.

Though the term friend in Hollywood means something different than everywhere else.

THE MURDER OF A STARLET

In this town, everyone's got an angle and Paul has more of them than an isosceles triangle.

He's the type of guy who, after you shake his hand, you check to see if you still have all your fingers.

But Max has to admit some of his schemes are good.

The Chippendales thing is a case in point.

Great idea, but the guys got lousy follow-through.

He feels kind of sorry for him, so what the hell? He'll hold the reception at his place, plus he likes Dorothy. She's sweet.

He met a lot of girls in his life when he was an actor on a hit TV show.

But he's never met anyone as genuinely kind and guileless as her.

When Max first met Dorothy, he asked Paul if he cared about her.

Paul said he did.

Max said, *then get her out of here and take her back to Vancouver, this town will destroy her.*

Instead, Paul married her, and now she's gonna be a Playboy Centrefold.

How a guy like him landed a girl like her is beyond Max.

When the newlyweds walk in, he shakes Paul's hand and slaps him on the back.

Max hugs Dorothy and asks how she's doing.

Busy, she tells him.

She complains about a headache she's had for weeks, probably stress.

It's not the most festive party Max has ever thrown.

There are a few people from Paul's side, including a doctor friend who gives the bride and groom Quaaludes.

Paul's father is there too, he wears a white suit and seems eager to have his picture taken with Paul's new bride.

Dorothy has just two guests, the Playmate of the Year from 1978, and her old roommate, Molly.

THE MURDER OF A STARLET

Molly moved out of the apartment she shared with Dorothy and Paul a few months back.

Paul scared her one night when he got mad and tipped over a table.

But she's loyal to Dorothy, so she's here.

Most conspicuously absenties is anyone from Dorothy's family.

She confesses they didn't come to the wedding, either.

She hasn't gotten up the nerve to tell them.

****

Ladies and gentlemen playboy Magazines 1979 Miss August Vancouver's own Dorothy Stratton.

Dorothy takes a big breath and flashes a dazzling smile, then runs out onto the stage.

She's in Jean shorts, a red polka dot halter top, and cowboy boots.

She gives the crowd a rock star away.

Her heart beats a mile a minute, but she's not nervous, not really, not anymore.

She's exhilarated.

It's July 1979, and Dorothy's on a cross-country tour of Canada to promote the August issue of the magazine.

And tonight is the Calgary Exhibition and Stampede.

It's an annual rodeo carnival and livestock fair, all in one and the fairgrounds are packed.

Paul stays home.

Playboy wants to keep the marriage a secret.

It's harder to fantasize about a beautiful girl if she has a husband by her side.

Instead, Playboy has sent a handler, her name is Elizabeth Norris.

She's the manager of publicity and doubles as a chaperone.

She knows how an avalanche of press can affect a girl who isn't ready, but Elizabeth is surprised at how quickly Dorothy takes to it.

She loves the crowd and the crowd loves her back.

She never tires of signing autographs.

When Elizabeth tries to pull her away, Dorothy smiles and says a little bit longer, people came out here to see me I can't let them down.

In July, Playboy releases the August issue and the magazine flies off the stand.

On the cover is Candy-loving the winner of the Great Playmate Hunt, and in the Centre on Page 116 is Dorothy's first Playboy spread.

Fifteen photographs, some black and white of Dorothy, clothed, half-clothed, and finally without any clothes at all.

The article is filled with quotes, and insights from Dorothy on who she is, what she wants, and what turns her on.

I'm a sucker for the romantic approach. I love taking walks in the warm rain. She confesses to being very shy and says she writes poetry to help her express her feelings. She even allowed Playboy to publish one of her poems.

Her goal, she says, is to become a successful actress. And it seems like her dream is starting to take form.

Playboy sets her up with an agent, David Wilder, who represents several playmates, but no one is quite like Dorothy.

Wilder will later say she was exactly what this town likes a beautiful girl who could act.

When a production company requests a playmate type for a small role in a movie called Americathon, Wilder sends Dorothy.

Another movie calls for a pretty girl who can skate, Dorothy skates like a pro.

They're just bit parts, but then Wilder calls with a lead, a movie called Autumn Born.

The part is about a 17-year-old rich orphan who was kidnapped and abused.

The script is lackluster, the director and actor are unknown, but it's the lead and they want Dorothy.

If she takes the role, it'll be a great learning experience.

She'll be acting in front of the camera.

It shoots in Vancouver, but she'll be back in no time.

THE MURDER OF A STARLET

A door has opened and Dorothy is walking through.

****

****

While Dorothy is in Canada shooting Autumn Born, Paul looks for a new apartment for the two of them.

He finds a brand new two-story stucco in West LA on West Clarkson Drive, just across from the 10 freeway.

It's bigger than anywhere they've lived and they decide to get a roommate.

A guy named Steve Kushner whom Dorothy met at the Playboy Club.

He's a laid-back live-and-let-live type and spends most of his time at his girlfriend's place, which suits Paul just fine.

Kushner takes the 2nd floor and Paul and Dorothy claim the downstairs.

Paul decorates the walls with photos of Dorothy.

His father helps him move in and then stays for a week.

Paul, is never much like the guy, but it feels good to see the approval in his dad's eyes.

See pop I told you I'd make it he thinks unlike you.

One day, when he and Paul are watching, his dad tells him he shut down his shop.

Times have been tough since then, he says.

He asks if Paul can give him a loan.

Paul knows he could swing it, but he turns them down.

Later, Paul tells one of his buddies he was surprised at how good it felt.

Imagine him telling his old man No.

As money starts rolling in, it's Paul who cashes the cheques and spends most of the money on himself.

He buys in 1974 Mercedes 450SE for $13,000, while Dorothy continues to drive her beat-up Mercury Cougar.

He puts custom plates on his car that says star80.

You're gonna get playmate in a year, I can smell it, he tells her, you're gonna be a star. The next Marilyn

Monroe, and then we'll move to Bel Air, where all the big movie producers live.

Dorothy smiles and nods, but privately she tells friends she's worried.

She feels like Paul is setting it up where she can't fail without failing them both.

Not that Paul would listen.

He's got a vision when he drinks too much, he likes to tell people their rocket ship to the moon is taking off.

To Dorothy, he says next year is our year baby, anything can happen.

THE MURDER OF A STARLET

CHAPTER 4

PLAYMATE OF THE YEAR

It's Monday, October 22nd, 1979 movie director Peter Bogdanovich is in the main hall of the Playboy Mansion when he hears someone call his name.

He turns towards the voice it's a tall girl with candy, red lips, and white blonde hair.

She's smiling hi, remember me? I'm Dorothy Stratton, we met last year.

He remembers.

She's not the kind of girl you forget.

He ran into her at a party here at the mansion last year.

She was with playmate candy-loving, but Peter only had eyes for Dorothy.

He would say later, she was the most beautiful woman he had ever seen.

This is saying a lot because Peter Bogdanovich had met some of the hottest women in Hollywood.

THE MURDER OF A STARLET

In the early 1970s, he had directed a string of hits, the last picture show, what's up doc? Paper moon

With it came fame and a pile of Oscars for his actress.

He left his wife and kids and moved in with his alleged new lead actress Cybill Shepherd.

But then came a string of flops, people were saying he was arrogant and difficult, and shouldn't have put his girlfriend in so many of his movies.

That's how fast this town turns on you.

Now Sybil is gone, and so are most of the offers.

He's alone has been, by Hollywood standards, at the age of 40.

But he hasn't given up, his last picture was a low-budget shot in Singapore and financed by Hef.

It got decent reviews, but virtually no distribution.

But he and Heffner struck up a friendship, that's why he came to the mansion.

Well, that and the girls.

THE MURDER OF A STARLET

When he met Dorothy that first time he gave her his number, and told her he was casting a picture, maybe she could read for him.

Oh, this line in the book.

He wasn't surprised she didn't call.

People in Hollywood can smell when you're down on your luck.

And since he and Sybil broke up, he knows he has a reputation for blowing through beautiful women, but here she is one year later looking at him with her dreamy eyes.

Of course, I remember you, he tells her, but not your hair is it different?

She admits that it is.

They dyed it, she tells him.

She leads them to a staircase and they sit down on the third step and start chatting like old friends.

She tells him about the movie she made in Canada, a low-budget feature, but she had a real part of the lead.

She's even excited about the smaller roles, Skatetown USA and Fantasy Island.

He's sure she's been through the casting mill plenty. It's not easy being a playmate. Most agents don't take girls who post nude. Seriously.

Yet Dorothy has an innocent quality like the town hasn't yet got to her.

The more she says, the more Peter is mesmerized.

But then she confesses and she's married.

Peter tries to hide his disappointment.

Are you happily married? he asks.

She avoids his eyes when she says there are some problems, but it is her fault.

Their conversation continues after dinner and this time it's Peter's turn to share.

When he speaks, he has a boyish Deb and air quality that matches his appearance and asks God, and a tented pair of tortoiseshell glasses.

He tells her about his new project, a comedy he made in New York.

He just finished this group this summer.

He's got financing and a plan to shoot in New York City in the spring.

When he stands up to leave, he says, why don't you read for a part?

And then he waits.

Finally, she says, I'd love to.

It's a small role he has in mind as a secretary who works at a detective agency.

More importantly, he thinks to himself, that means he'll get to see her again, assuming she doesn't change her mind, she'll call her agent in the morning.

As he watches her walk back into the mansion living room, Peter somehow knows Dorothy Stratton is going to be in his life.

****

It's a weekend in October 1979, Hugh Hefner sits at a table by his pool playing backgammon.

THE MURDER OF A STARLET

ABC TV has set up cameras along the driveway and on the roof of the mansion.

There are cameras at the front door inside the entryway and on either side of the swimming pool.

If a playmate is doing something, the cameraman captures it on film.

It's all part of a TV shoot for a new Playboy special on ABC that Hef is calling, the roller disco and pajama party.

The special will give people at home and inside a peek into what it's like to attend a weekend party at the mansion.

Game show host Richard Dawson is acting as M.C., taking the viewers around the mansion.

He'll introduce the viewers to Hef, there will be parties and skits and interviews with celebrities.

And oodles of sexy playmates, cavorting and swimsuits, as they skate and swam and dance.

Peter Bogdanovich attended one of those events the previous year and promised himself never again

But would Hef called him personally and asked him to be one of the background extras for some pajama party shots, he agreed.

He figures maybe he'll get a chance to see Dorothy again.

When he arrives at the Playboy Mansion wearing pajamas, a blue robe, and slippers, the party is thinning out.

But he sees Dorothy heading into the TV room to watch footage from the week before.

Her arm is linked to Hef's.

Peter follows them inside.

The room is filled with network execs and a few partygoers.

Dorothy sits alone on a chair, hands folded on her lap.

Heffner pops the VHS tape into the deck and presses play.

Images of the partygoers play across the screen, dozens of people dancing, laughing, and drinking.

Cutaways of Hef show him at the back right table in the middle of three blondes and low-cut tops.

It's just another day in his life.

There were dozens of shots of Dorothy.

It's the first time Peter has seen Dorothy on film and he's hypnotised.

The camera loves her, even in a large group of people, his eyes find her.

He's amazed by how much she does with so few lines.

Each time he sees her, there's a subtle difference in the way she moves or speaks.

The tape ends, Hef pops it out and leads the group out to the Great Hall, where everybody buzzed about how great it's going to be.

Peter stays in the background, by the time he has a chance to speak with Hef, Dorothy has gone home.

Footage looks good, he tells Hef.

Hef agrees.

It swings, he says, and the blonde, Peter says she's....

He searches for the word pauses for a while and finally says, Interesting.

Peter tells Hef he may have a part for her in his new film.

Hef nods.

You should come for the rest of the taping; he suggests we think she's got something special. It's an invitation, Peter can't resist.

****

The next afternoon, Dorothy is doing her best to hold down a wiggly squirrel.

James Kahn is trying not to make her laugh.

They're filming a skit for the ABC special in the backyard of the mansion, and this is the last day of shooting.

Hef is also given Dorothy a running gag with Richard Dawson that plays over a live performance by Chuck Mangione.

She spots Peter Bogdanovich standing on the sidelines.

THE MURDER OF A STARLET

He flashes her big smile and waves; she smiles back.

When the crew stops the action to reset the camera, Peter finds her near the pool, he's hesitant, almost shy.

If you feel like talking. I'll be over on the cushions with friends, he says.

Dorothy tells him she's working.

I feel like I'm in every shot, she says.

That night at the dance party, the cameraman set up for the final shot, another concert with Chuck Mangione, this time underneath the stars next to the mansion fire-lit pool, and Dorothy has a final scene with Richard Dawson where he finally gets the girl.

****

Peter Bogdanovich will look back on November 1st, 1979, as a day that changed his life and brought back his muse.

It's sunny and warm like any other day in Los Angeles, but when he opens the door, it's like a ray of light comes streaming in.

Dorothy is here to read for him.

She's wearing a thin white cotton dress and big straw hat and tall strappy heels that make her teeter when she walks.

It's like she stepped out of the 1800s, surrounded by a soft, gauzy veil, or maybe it's just the romantic in him.

Come in, come in, have a seat anywhere, Peter says as she invites Dorothy inside.

She chooses a tan leather armchair.

Now let's have some tea, Peter said.

Peter finds tea, relaxes him, the ritual, the propriety of it all.

It seems to relax Dorothy too, and break the ice.

Peter brings out a copy of the script and begins to tell her more about the movie.

It's called **They All Laughed**, it's a romantic comedy set in New York City. There's a firm of private detectives who fall for the cheating wives of their suspicious clients, but it's a real love story.

The role he has in mind for her is Amy, she's the firm secretary and she's secretly in love with her boss.

He hands her the script and explains there aren't many lines, not yet, but just read it the way she thinks the character is.

He's pleased when she adds nuance that makes the humor come through.

She's naturally, he thinks.

But what strikes him the most is how genuine she is in a town of superficial people, Dorothy is real.

After the reading, Peter doesn't want her to go, so he picks up a copy of one of his favorite plays, Private Lives by Noël Coward.

He tells her the story:

" A divorced couple shows up at the same hotel with new spouses and soon find themselves alone in the moonlight while an orchestra plays their favorite song", Peter sings a couple of lines *"Someday I'll find you moonlight behind you"*.

It's a classic 1950s ballad that brings Peter back to a simpler time.

When Peter is done, Dorothy smiles and suddenly it feels like the room is warmer and brighter.

Wonderful, she says.

When the teapot is empty, Peter offers Dorothy a cigarette and they both smoke in silence.

Paul doesn't let me smoke, she tells him, I have to sneak them when he's not around.

Officially, I'm not a smoker either, he says.

They both laugh.

When Dorothy says she has to go to a Playboy shoot across town Peter walks her to her car and olive green, 67 cougars.

She thanked him for the opportunity and held out her hand.

Peter says *I'd like it if you came back to read some of the other scenes.*

Dorothy says she'd like that.

He doesn't tell her there are no other scenes yet, he's going to write them and expand the part for her, he also doesn't tell her he's smitten.

THE MURDER OF A STARLET

****

It's late November and Playboy photo editor Moe Grabowski sits in her office.

Dorothy sits across from her.

She looks stunned, her hands covering her mouth like she can't believe what she just heard.

Moe laughs, are you OK?

Dorothy nods, it just took a moment to sink in, I can't believe it's me.

Believe it, Moe says, Playmate of the Year Dorothy Stratten.

The decision was Hef, of course.

Hef always knew Dorothy had potential, but she had to find the poise and confidence to handle the press, the appearances, and the fans, and Dorothy exceeded their expectations.

Playmate of the Year, I just feel so special.

You deserve it, Moe tells her.

Her August photo spread got more fan mail than any other playmate that year, and the press tour that followed earned her even more fans.

What's different about Dorothy is that none of this has gone to her head.

She still has no idea how special she is.

She never expects things to be given to her or takes anything for granted.

Now she's on her way to becoming a star.

The two hug each other tightly, and Dorothy starts to cry, happy tears.

Moe tells her she'll have to get back to work right away on the photo spread.

The issue comes out in June, there'll be an award ceremony at the mansion and a month-long press tour.

And then there are the prizes, $25,000 in cash, the brand-new Jaguar, and a brass-lined bathtub.

The total package comes to more than $200,000.

It's more money than Dorothy's ever dreamed of, she can't wait to tell Paul.

****

Paul Schneider maneuvers his Mercedes through traffic on the 405.

I should have taken Westwood, he complains, the 405 always sucks.

It's late in the day and already dark, the cars on the freeway forming under less strain of the greenlights the curl into Infinity.

Dorothy tells them they have time and she's not going to Peter Bogdanovich's house for another hour.

When Dorothy told Paul about the part, he wasn't surprised.

That the Playmate of the Year Jackpot, he didn't realize it would be quite that much, 200K in money and prizes.

He's already spending it in his mind.

Another car, and a new house, put some into a business.

THE MURDER OF A STARLET

Listen, Paul, Dorothy said, I was thinking.

He looks at her face, he knows that expression, she doesn't think he's going to like what she's about to say and he doesn't, she says someone a Playboy recommended a business manager, some big shark guy who managed the money of Farrah Fawcett and Warren Beatty.

I'm your manager, he says.

But this is a lot of money, Paul, he could invest it for us.

It would leave you more time to manage my career.

Paul thinks about it; she has a point as long as he can still sign the cheques.

Alright, let's see what he has to say, he tells her.

She motions to the right, that's the turn.

Paul pulls into a long driveway and then stops in front of a large Spanish-style house.

He let out a low whistle and said nice joint.

So this is what it's like to live in Bel Air? Paul asked how long she'd be; he had things to do.

THE MURDER OF A STARLET

Not long, she says, I'm just reading a few more scenes.

She opens the door and then turns back, wish me luck, Paul Winks at her and tells her, you don't need luck, baby, you got me.

****

Dorothy loves talking about acting with Peter.

She's still so new to the craft and he seems to know so much.

He tells her he's protective of actors he also tells her he's expanding the part of Amy.

Something about that makes Dorothy feel hopeful, maybe that means he thinks she's right for the role, but it won't be official until there's an offer.

When they're done talking about the script, Peter says he wants to show her something.

It's sort of an astrology book.

Peter says he got it from a friend, it's an unusual book that explains an old occult science and connects certain cards to people's birthdays.

Peter tells her he's a Jack of Hearts.

What's your birthday? He asks.

She tells him February 28th.

Ohh, you're the 10 Of clubs, he says.

He flips to the back of the book to see the yearly predictions.

He tells her there's a chart that shows which people will be important in your life each year.

Peter is 40 years old.

He moves his finger across the page.

Look at that, he says, your card is next to mine.

Dorothy's excited about the game.

Where's Paul? She asks.

His birthday is April 15th.

Six of Diamonds, Peter says.

Then he flips back to his chart, the three cards are lined up next to each other, Dorothy's delighted.

Look at that, she says.

THE MURDER OF A STARLET

Then Peter jumps to his chart at age 41.

Now both Dorothy and Paul's cards are gone.

She looks at Peter and asks, what does it mean?

Peter slams the book shut. Who knows? It's just silly, he says.

Dorothy smiles.

She has to go Paul is waiting.

****

Business manager Robert Houston works with a lot of Hollywood types and the first thing he tells them is how important it is to save for a rainy day.

Not all the firm's clients are crazy success stories like Paul Newman or Goldie Hawn's.

Fame and fortune are fleeting, he's seen it too many times in Hollywood.

A person lucks into a hit TV show or movie and they think the money will never stop flowing until it does.

It's December 1979, when he sits down with Dorothy Stratten and her husband Paul Snider.

It's not how he pictured a playmate.

Sure, she's a knockout, but she's also level-headed and smart.

She tells him she wants to be responsible with the money coming in, and puts some away for her future.

Her husband, however, has different ideas.

Look, Bob, he says *if there's one thing I know you need to spend money to make money, and I got a lot of ideas in the pipeline. If I invest early in theoretically bigger payout later, but I've been reading this book, the only investment guide you'll ever need.*

Houston listens to Paul's theories and his plan for Dorothy's brand, he keeps emphasizing the word Partners, and he makes it clear he should have an equal say over Dorothy's finances and half her income.

Dorothy doesn't say much of anything out loud, but Houston notices her shift uncomfortably in her seat.

Then she shoots him a very subtle side-to-side head shake.

He's seen this before with couples where the wife is the star, he knows the language and she wants him to humor Schneider and not make any waves.

Houston follows her lead.

He says he'll look into the paperwork and research tax laws.

Paul nods.

Well, let's get this wrapped up soon.

Houston makes some mental note to call Dorothy later when they can talk in private.

He also makes a mental note to look into Schneider to see if he has any income of his own.

Lately, Moe Grabowski has noticed that Dorothy hasn't been herself.

They've been shooting the Playmate of the Year pictorial for a few weeks, and every morning Dorothy arrives looking exhausted.

Her eyes are puffy like she's been crying.

THE MURDER OF A STARLET

Sometimes she's late and Dorothy is never late.

Moe thinks she knows the source of it all too, Paul Schneider.

He calls the studio non-stop, demanding to speak to her.

When Dorothy takes his calls, Moe can hear her pleading and arguing.

When she hangs up the phone, she often retreats to her dressing room in tears.

Through the door, she can hear Dorothy crying.

Moe Peaks in her head through the door and asks, are you OK, honey? anything you want to talk about?

Dorothy shakes her head; I think I'm just tired I feel out of sorts.

Whatever is going on, Moe doesn't want to pressure her.

To cheer her up, Moe buys her a Shih Tzu puppy.

It seems to work.

Dorothy names the dog Marsdon, Hef's middle name, and shows him off at the mansion.

THE MURDER OF A STARLET

She even poses with the dog in one of the photos for Playmate of the Year.

Later that week, Moe asks her how the puppy is doing.

Dorothy tells her that he's always with Paul and she doesn't get a chance to play with him much.

Three days later, Moe asks about the dog again, this time, Dorothy looks upset, and she tells her Marston died.

Moe asked what happened, but Dorothy shuts down.

Moe has her suspicions, whatever happened to that dog Paul had something to do with it.

Maybe a weekend away, just to relax will do Dorothy some good away from work away from Paul.

Moe takes Dorothy to a spa in La Costa, near San Diego.

They play tennis, get massages, and lounge by the pool, it's a stress-free weekend.

Dorothy comes back 5 pounds lighter; she seems like she's back to her happy upbeat self.

THE MURDER OF A STARLET

Moe just hopes the feeling will last now that she's back in Paul's orbit.

****

It's early January 1980 and movie director William Sachs is looking for a hit. He's 37 and he's written and directed a string of low-budget movies.

Some are even considered cult classics like The Incredible Melting Man, about an astronaut who eats human flesh to stay alive, after returning to Earth.

Mostly he's called to fix other people's Scripts.

It's a living but he doesn't get screen credit.

What he wants is to make his films, genre stretching, laggard movies, just like his hero's director Fellini Luau.

Sachs thinks he's got a chance to make a mark with his new script, GALAXINA.

He originally conceived it as a Western, but it's since evolved.

Now it's a tongue-in-cheek spoof, a nod to the sci-fi movie craze that hit a fever pitch with Star Wars.

Who knows, maybe this is the one that will make him famous.

But first, he's got a string of problems to solve, the bane of every Hollywood director.

He's supposed to start shooting in just a few days, but his sets were almost destroyed in a bad rainstorm and he still hasn't found an actress to play GALAXINA, the female robot at the center of the movie.

Of course, she has to be beautiful, but she also has to play a robot, There is not a lot of dialogue, so you think it is easy but it's not.

Sachs producer Maryland Tensor has auditioned more than 300 actresses, some of the most beautiful women in town, some are wooden, some are too emotional, and not one has hit the bullseye.

He's starting to wonder if she even exists, even here in Hollywood.

Then he gets a call from Agent David Wilder about Playboy model Dorothy Stratten.

Sachs tells him to bring her in.

THE MURDER OF A STARLET

When Dorothy walks in two days later with her agent, Sachs is standing in one of the back production offices, and she's wearing black slacks and a white gaze blouse in her high heels, she seems 10 feet tall.

About 20 people are running around or sitting at desks.

Everyone stopped their work to check her out, including Sachs.

Sachs, will later Say, *"There are plenty of beautiful women. It wasn't only that was something else. Maybe people call it star quality. It was nasty, real kind of thing it was amazing and it was a perfect woman"*.

For Sachs, it's not about line reading, it's about getting to know the person, especially for this part.

So he asks Dorothy about herself.

She tells him about where she's from and how long she's been in L.A., but she doesn't have to say anything.

Sachs already knows Dorothy Stratten is GALEXINA.

****

Dorothy feels like a new woman when she gets home.

And then she gets the call from David Wilder, the one she's been waiting for.

It's official, Peter Bogdonavich, wants her in and they all laughed.

She goes a little crazy at that moment, screaming and yelling.

He told her he was writing some new scenes, but turns out he created a whole new character for her name, Dolores.

It's bigger than the original secretary's role.

The film is scheduled to shoot in New York at the end of March, a few days after Galaxina wraps, she's going to be busy.

She calls her new business manager, Bob Houston, for advice.

How should she manage all this new income?

He advises her to set up a corporation in her name, they'll call it in. Dorothy Stratten Enterprises will own 100% of the stock.

The corporation will pay Dorothy's salary which will be deposited into a joint checking account.

Both Paul and Dorothy can sign for these funds, but only Dorothy will be able to draw from the income of the corporation.

She knows Paul won't be happy about the new arrangement, but this time she's determined to follow her business manager's advice.

She has to look out for her family in Canada and her future.

When she tells Paul what she's done, he's angry, and they fight.

He berated her for taking management advice from anyone other than him.

Do you think they have your best interest at heart Dorothy? they are sharks, he says, everyone in Hollywood is out for themselves, I'm looking out for you.

But Dorothy stands firm.

There's plenty of money in the joint account, she tells him, I'm not trying to hide money from you, Paul, this is just the way it's done.

She can tell he's not satisfied, but what can he do?

Paul never likes it when other men horn in his business.

He's been burned too many times, and in his mind, Dorothy Stratten Enterprises belongs to him.

The fancy suit in the Beverly Hills office may know more about tax loopholes, but he knows more about Dorothy, what she can do, and how far she can go. She still has tickets to the big time and he's going to make the most of it.

Now that the money is starting to come in, Paul is expanding his marketing plans for the Dorothy brand.

And he has an idea that could bring it big bucks, a poster, just like Farrah had.

He pictures Dorothy on roller skates with a sexy disco-style bodysuit, something high cotton, glittering, lots of cleavages, and a little bow tie choker as the bunnies wear.

Now he just needs a photographer and he's got the perfect team in mind.

A couple he met last summer named Bill and Susan Letracy.

They are a husband and wife team just like he and Dorothy, and he likes their work.

Woodinville picks up the phone, Paul starts rigging, *Bill my man, It's Paul Snider I have excellent news, We're moving forward with the poster*, Paul says he's got it all worked out.

He figures at least a million copies and each night at least a cool 300 grand and that's just a start.

As Dorothy's career blows, more people want it shall be the fantasy of teenage boys around the world, they just need to work out the particulars and schedule the shoot.

He's got a few more ideas about where that came from.

He wants to do a book in two books, one will be a coffee table book, Photos of Dorothy. John Derek did it when he married Beau, not actress with the cornrows. Derek took the photos himself.

He's going to pitch John on doing one of those books on Dorothy.

He's also going to write his book, a biography about his life and how he discovered Dorothy.

He has already found a writer; he just needs to give him deposit money for the first draught.

Dorothy is not the only one who's going to get attention, Paul Schneiders's name is going to be famous too, you can take that to the bank.

****

It's late January, just after dawn on a chilly day in Malibu, California.

Dorothy sits in the makeup chair on the set of GALAXINA, sipping a strong black coffee.

Peter thought she should pass on the movie, but everyone told her she should do it.

Her agent said it's a great opportunity, the title role in an American film.

She has to admit it's fun with the makeup, the costumes, the set.

Her part doesn't have many lines, for the first half of the movie, she doesn't say anything at all.

But that's what makes it a different kind of challenge.

She'll have to emote with her face and her body, it's a chance to get better at her craft.

Dorothy's stylist fusses with her hair.

Oh Oh, she says.

Dorothy looks up.

The woman's holding a thick clump of white blonde hair in her hands.

Oh God, it's gotten worse, Dorothy moans.

Her hair has been in awful shape since she started bleaching it for Playboy last year.

Recently she noticed it coming out in the sink and big patches.

The hairstylist confers with Sachs. The director says they'll have to go with a blonde wig. Dorothy's embarrassed, but she gets it, you can have a patchy-haired GALAXINA.

As the stylist gets to work, Dorothy turns back to the script.

THE MURDER OF A STARLET

The movie takes place in the year 3008, somewhere in deep space. It's about a handsome crewman who falls in love with a robot pilot and tries to reprogram her to become a real woman. Her name is GALAXINA Dorothy's role.

She's got her work cut out for her.

She'll have to imagine herself as a robot and then transform into a robot who's developing human feelings.

Director Bill Sachs welcomes her input.

He watches her performance closely and compliments her at the end of her scenes, telling her she's a natural.

She likes Bill, he's a sweet guy with an even temperament never blows up or yells.

Paul Drives her to the set and picks her up.

It's a haul of more than 20 miles each way.

Some days he even dropped by at lunch and hung out.

It makes Dorothy feel self-conscious.

THE MURDER OF A STARLET

She tells him, he doesn't have to be there, but he just says *you're part of my job and I gotta make sure I'm watching the talent.*

The days Paul doesn't come to say he finds reasons to call.

If Dorothy is shooting, he calls again. It puts her on edge and sometimes she cries, She's so sick of crying. Why can't Paul just be happy for them?

He always wants to know when the shooting will wrap and if it runs late, he gets upset.

I don't know why he wants me at home, Dorothy confides to one of the other actors, when I get there, he'll be out at a nightclub somewhere, she says.

****

Director Bill Sachs hears the familiar sound, of boots on concrete.

There's a grading, Jing Jing Jin, when the Spurs hit the stage, one of the crew Mumbles under his breath saying, Jesus, here comes.

It's Paul Schneider again, every time he shows up, Dorothy stops whatever she's doing and freezes.

He always wants to hang around and shoot the shit.

One time Sachs was talking to JD Hendon, one of the stars.

He's got an issue of Playboy open door, the centerfold, he overhears Schneider say, doesn't she have great talent, no wonder Dorothy can't concentrate when Schneiders here.

Often when Sachs calls Dorothy home, it's always Paul who picks up the phone.

Sachs is always polite, introduces himself, asks to speak to Dorothy, and he's always met with silence.

Hello, the same silence, *it's Sachs, you know the director?*

finally, he will hear Schneider's voice, *Yeah, I know you are.*

That's it.

Then there's a gauntlet and before Paul will put Dorothy on the phone, he's got a picture of something. Usually, it's a documentary on the Chippendales dancers.

THE MURDER OF A STARLET

See Bill, I got aligned with the guy who manages these guys. I was the one who came up with the concept, were not in business....

Sachs is often held captive for half an hour to a time before Schneider gets Dorothy on the line.

One day, Dorothy arrives on sits in tears as Paul screeches off.

Later, lunch Sachs Jackson on her, she's embarrassed.

I know it looks bad, but my husband loves me, she says, he will do anything for me. He has me up on a pedestal.

The director has no idea why Dorothy defends him or stays with him.

Sure, he can be charming, he's not bad looking if you just go by the skin suit, but inside the guy is cold, always standing in the corner with his back to the wall, staring at everyone with those cold, dead eyes. Snyder gives him the Heebie Jeebies.

Peter Bogdanovich feels like he's on fire again they all laughed at full speed ahead.

He has all the major roles cast, Ben Gazzara in the lead, Audrey Hepburn as the wife of a European tycoon, and Dorothy as Dolores Martin.

As he rewrote the script, he realized Dorothy was capable of much more than a small secretary part.

So he introduced a new role, a young blonde whose marriage is in trouble with Dorothy as his muse, the part practically writes itself.

He's been flying back and forth between New York and LA since December, location scouts casting smaller roles, and approving sets and wardrobe.

When he's home, he meets with Dorothy, helps her practice her lines, and explains to her how he envisions Dolores.

The last time he felt this kind of juice was when he directed his last movie in the last picture show, there's something about helping to find the part, it's like creating a person, and the more he sees in Dorothy, the more smitten he gets.

He'll later say falling in love with your actresses an occupational hazard if you are the director.

One Sunday in late January he and Dorothy managed to get away from their hectic schedules and spend an afternoon by the ocean.

They park near a deserted beach and walk down an incline and onto the warm sand.

Dorothy takes off her heels and swings them by the strap.

This feels nice, she says.

Peter takes her hand and they walk in silence.

It feels natural to wrap his arm around her waist and feel her arm in a circle.

And then they are kissing just like that, it feels like the most natural thing in the world to do, and it's exactly how Peter imagined it would be.

It feels like they're inside a cocoon, no one or nothing else there.

And then Peters back on a plane back to New York to move the movie train forward again.

It almost feels like a dream.

And then he gets a postcard, it's from Dorothy, it says :

" *Dear Peter, One day since yesterday, Love Dorothy*".

When they meet again two weeks later, it's like they share a secret, but Peter doesn't want it to be a secret.

He's uneasy about the fact that Dorothy is still married, he knows she's not the kind of woman who would do this with just anyone.

Paul is only the second person she's been with in her life, but he wants more.

He can tell Dorothy feels it too, she tells him, *it's just too difficult to be intimate and then goes back to Paul I just can't do it.*

He won't force Dorothy to choose between him and Paul, but he wants to know where they stand.

He tells her the truth, he's falling for her, but it's going to be hard until she decides to leave Paul.

Dorothy tells him she's torn; she says she feels sorry for Paul.

THE MURDER OF A STARLET

I still love him, she says, but it isn't the same anymore, I feel so bad. I don't know what's wrong.

Peter doesn't understand.

Why would she settle when she could have the world?

When he flies back to New York, he tells her he won't see her again until rehearsals in March.

Then they'll be in New York together, it's going to be a long month.

When Galaxina wraps, Dorothy is excited for a new adventure.

She has a part in a movie with a major director, a man she is falling for who brings out her best.

Paul wants to go with her, but Dorothy tells him it's not possible.

As she packs, he watches her, his eyes shift between irritation and desperation.

It's a closed set, she explains, it won't be like Galaxina it will be shooting on location all over the place.

She doesn't tell him that Peter would never tolerate Paul popping in whenever he feels like it.

Paul has no choice, he backs down, but he makes her promise she will call, she promises. And answer the phone when I call you, he says, I have stuff going on, too.

Maybe they just need a break some time away from each other to help her work things out in her head and get some clarity on what she should do.

But right now, she's gotta stay focused, she's going to New York.

When Dorothy gets on the plane, she has butterflies in her stomach. She has no idea what to expect.

She hasn't felt like this since the first time she flew to LA for the 25th anniversary test shoot, that was her very first flight.

It amazes her to think about what she wrote on her application, how she hoped the Playboy experience would help her gain more confidence in herself.

She wrote that her dream was to become a star of sorts.

That was less than two years ago and everything happened so fast.

Now she has a real role with smart lines in a real movie.

She's just celebrated her 20th birthday, feels like a new chapter is starting in her life and she can't wait to see what happens next.

CHAPTER 5

RISING STAR

Peter Bogdanovich nervously paces the terminal at JFK Airport, wondering where Dorothy is.

It's March 22nd, 1980, just after 9:00 PM.

She flew first class, so she should be one of the first off the plane, but she's not.

Peter doesn't see her in the second or third group of passengers either.

Maybe she missed the flight, or maybe changed her mind.

Peter turns away from the terminal.

Did she get the gate wrong? He asks himself.

And then he looks back one more time, and there she is.

Even with her hair disheveled and teetering on her high heels, Dorothy Stratten is stunning.

She carries two suitcases of purses and a large shopping bag.

It makes her look like a kid who just ran away from home. O

h my God it took forever to get these out of the overhead bin and I have four more, she says.

He grabs her bags and they head to baggage claim as she continues chattering excitedly, *I think I took all of my clothes, even Paul said it looked like I was moving out.*

Paul is her husband, Peter hasn't met him, but Dorothy told him enough to know that Paul wouldn't be happy seeing his wife leave for three weeks.

He wanted to come to New York, but Peter said not.

Peter is just glad she's here, he pretends to focus on the carousel to avoid looking at her like some Love-struck kid.

He drops Dorothy at the Wyndham Hotel on 58th St in Manhattan so she can check in and get settled.

They make a plan to meet at Peters Hotel.

An hour later, Dorothy knocked on his door when she walked in, he gave her a tour.

It's a penthouse suite with a marble fireplace and mirrors framed in 14-karat gold leaf.

Upstairs is a terrace overlooking Central Park.

Dorothy is delighted, it's like a room for a king, she said.

Peter tells where the studio pays for it, one of the perks of the job.

The two watched the sunset from the hotel balcony and it began to snow.

Dorothy tilts her face towards the sky, *it's so beautiful*, Dorothy said.

Inside they share a long kiss and then have an intimate dinner at a restaurant Uptown.

They talk about everything about Dorothy's family in Canada, Peter's life, and the role of Dolores, which Peter wrote just for her.

What they don't talk about is Paul or that Peter is in love with her.

At the end of the night, Dorothy tells him she's going to sleep in her room, and Peter understands.

The next day they meet up and walk through Central Park, and that evening they Make Love for the first time.

For Peter, it's one of the most magical moments of his life.

He'll look back on it and say he couldn't believe she existed, but she wasn't a dream.

When he wakes up, Dorothy is gone, but she's left a message and soap on the bathroom mirror, a little heart with an arrow through it.

He'll leave it there for the next two months.

Peter feels like he's starting a new life.

The only thing casting a shadow on the future is Dorothy's husband, Paul.

****

Dorothy has been in New York for almost 2 weeks and she's in love with the city.

THE MURDER OF A STARLET

The bustling energy of crowds moving through the streets and subways is like a choreographed ballet.

Yellow cabs, buses, and cars speed through the streets.

She's never seen so many Street vendors all selling something delicious, hot pretzels with mustard, hot dogs with the works.

Her days on the set are exciting, she doesn't have many lines her first week, but Peter lets her come to set and watch.

They're shooting in the streets of Manhattan in the center of the action.

All the actors in the cast are people she's only seen in TV or the movies.

Now she drinks coffee with John Ritter and watches Ben Gazzara laughing with Colleen Camp.

And then there's Audrey Hepburn, Dorothy still can't believe she's in a film with the actress who played Holly lightly in Breakfast at Tiffany's.

She has to pinch herself to believe that it's real.

And Peters in the centre of it all conferring with the DP, rewriting pages huddled with the actors and occasionally looking over at her and smiling.

Today, they're shooting in a bookstore.

Dorothy watches as Hepburn walks through the store, looking back and forth, as if browsing through the stacks.

A private detective played by Ben Gazzara follows behind her.

Suddenly, Hepburn looks up at him with a hint of a smile, she knows he's there.

Dorothy's amazed.

It's like Hepburn can show what she's thinking without saying a word.

When Dorothy is sure no one's watching, she silently mimics the star's elegant mannerisms.

Peters, known as an actor's director creates a safe space for them to get into character and try things out.

Dorothy loves watching him work he gets a spark of inspiration and makes it happen.

He's so different from Paul, who gets an idea but can't seem to follow through.

But lately, Paul hasn't been doing much of anything.

His only focus is on Dorothy and her career, he calls her every night at her hotel.

If he gets there, he'll keep her on the phone, badgering her with questions or asking for money.

If she doesn't pick up, he keeps calling, he even calls during the day, even though she told him she'd be on set.

He leaves messages at the front desk, *saying that her husband called.*

She takes Valium to calm her nerves, it helps when she tries to concentrate on her work.

Late one night, Paul calls about the roller-skating poster they shot a few months back.

Dorothy in a red high-cut skating outfit in red skates.

Paul figures they can sell a million copies and net a cool 300K.

He wants to know when she can look at them.

THE MURDER OF A STARLET

He needs her to pick one and sign the release form.

Dorothy tells Paul her days are so busy; can it wait until she's back?

Paul insists they need to move forward with this ASAP.

Gotta strike while the iron is hot timing is everything with these things, he says.

Dorothy says she'll need to get back to him.

When are you coming home? He wants to know.

A couple more weeks, it'll fly by, I promise, Dorothy replied.

Paul doesn't say anything.

One of the many ways he shows disapproval.

Finally, Dorothy says it's late Paul I need to study my lines. H

He pretends not to hear her.

I think we should buy a house and start thinking about kids, Paul says.

We can talk about it when I'm back.

Dorothy tries to deflect, but she knows she doesn't want kids with Paul.

I love you, he says.

Dorothy let out a breath and said *goodnight, Paul.*

After she hangs up, she walks over to Peters Hotel, where she spends the night, he makes her feel safe.

Dorothy's torn, she knows she's fallen for Peter, but she feels loyalty toward Paul, something has to give.

Paul shuffles through a stack of mail at the West Clarkson House, mostly bills, and then he spots an envelope with Dorothy's name.

He rips it open and finds a $2000 cheque from the Galaxina production company.

It's made out to Dorothy Stratten Enterprises, just what he's been waiting for.

He's already run through the money in the joint account, now he's scrambling for cash.

He goes to the bank almost every day to check if there are any new deposits into Dorothy's corporate account, but without Dorothy, the tellers are starting to give him attitude.

THE MURDER OF A STARLET

Paul shoves the cheque in his wallet and makes a phone call, he's got a plan to make sure the two grand will be in his hands before tonight.

A couple of hours later, Paul stands outside the Union Bank in Century City with the brunette, the girl he met at a club a few nights ago.

OK, You just walk in there and show him the cheque and say you're Dorothy, don't make a big deal out of it, Paul said.

The brunette shoots him a look and says *you already explained it to me 1000 times I got it.*

Paul walks inside at the teller window, he's all smiles.

When the girl doesn't say anything, he nudges her and said Dorothy *sweetheart, give the lady the cheque.*

The girl does what she's told.

The Teller examines the cheque. turns it over and then pushes the cheque back to him and she says *Dorothy Stratten is a blonde, your friend has brown hair.*

Paul grits his teeth leans into the window and says to the teller lady look, *I'm Dorothy's husband we have a joint account here I need you to cash this now.*

This was written in Dorothy Stratten Enterprises; she says flatly only Dorothy can cash cheques on that account.

Paul snatches the cheque, grabs the brunette by the arm, and storms out of the bank.

Back in the car, Paul Jams his foot down hard on the accelerator.

How can Dorothy do this to him after everything he's done for her 50/50? That was their deal, and now she's trying to Welch.

Paul knows he won't be able to reach her today, he's on set all day shooting.

But there's something he can't do right now.

As soon as he gets home, he's calling Houston.

Robert Houston looks up from his desk to see his secretary's agitated face.

It's Paul Snyder on the line. Again, I'm sorry, but he insists on speaking to you and says it's an emergency.

Houston is Dorothy's business manager, but a lot of his job these days seems to be fending off her husband.

Every day is an emergency for Paul Snyder.

It's OK I'll talk to him, Houston says.

Paul, what can I do for you? Houston ask,

Schneider wastes no time and said, *Listen, Bob, Dorothy's changed her mind. She wants me to own half the stock at Dorothy Stratten Enterprises. I need to be appointed as an officer so my name can be added to the corporate account.*

OK, Paul, Bob says I'll run it by Dorothy and get back to you.

What the hell Bob?

Schneider is shouting now.

You're managing both of us, not just Dorothy we're a package deal, we share everything.

But Houston doesn't burg.

Look, Paul, I need to talk to Dorothy and as you know, she's shooting in New York, but I'll get back to you, Houston says.

Two days later, Paul now shows up in person, he's insistent.

Bob, we've got to do it, this is the way it's gotta be we're partners in this thing, she shares 50% of my income and I share 50% in hers.

Houston knows Paul has no income of his own, the only thing he has is Dorothy, and he's not even her agent.

Later, when Houston gets Dorothy on the phone, she doesn't seem surprised that Paul is being so aggressive.

That's just how he is she says.

But she agrees not to add him as an officer of Stratten Enterprises.

Houston says, I just don't see how two people can fight so hard over money and still be together romantically.

THE MURDER OF A STARLET

He's surprised by her response.

She says sadly, *Bob there hasn't been a romantic relationship between Paul and me in over a year.*

Houston doesn't say anything about what he thinks Paul Schneider is going to get one hell of a wake-up call.

In mid-April, Dorothy flies back to Los Angeles during a break in the filming, she'll be gone for almost a month on a publicity tour for her Playmate of the Year Issue.

Playboy has all sorts of appearances planned.

It will kick off with an announcement at the mansion given by Hefner himself, followed by a spot on Johnny Carson, after that a two-week tour across Canada, then it's back to New York to finish the movie.

She feels like she's caught up in an exciting whirlwind each day, brighter than the next

It would be perfect except for Paul.

When Dorothy gets back to their apartment on West Clarkson Rd, he wants her attention to be focused on him and then half the time he's not even there.

One day she takes him to a mansion party, but after they get there, he barely talks to her.

Instead, he flirts with other playmates while Dorothy sits quietly in the corner talking with friends.

When she looks up she sees Paul in the pool, he's got on a tight Speedo-style suit and he's flexing his muscles.

He's laughing too loud and drinking too much.

Someone later tells Dorothy he was handing out his number, telling the girls he manages playmates, and using her name.

I discovered Dorothy Stratten, he says, *I can do the same for you, you're just as hot.*

Dorothy figures it's his way of punishing her.

At home he's always ranting about something, telling her she's putting on weight.

He criticizes her clothes and forbids her from wearing jeans, and then there's the money, always the money.

He says it isn't fair that he's not part of Stratten Enterprises, he seems so unhappy.

THE MURDER OF A STARLET

Dorothy suggests maybe they should take a break separate for a while his face tightens, and he says to Dorothy, *If you walk out that door, you can never come back.*

It scares Dorothy it reminds her of when her father left home.

Paul knows how much that hurt her, which makes it worse.

Dorothy hates the way she lets him get to her, she's ashamed of how much they fight, and she keeps her feelings private out of embarrassment.

But one day she opens up to her friend Luann.

Luann has always been friendly and warm to Dorothy.

She was miss June and Dorothy, Miss August, and she knows Paul well.

Her boyfriend Chip is one of Paul's only friends, they all used to double date.

One morning they're driving to exercise class and Dorothy just blurts it out and said *I'm so unhappy, I don't know what to do about Paul, he makes me so nervous.*

THE MURDER OF A STARLET

She pulls out a cigarette and lights up.

Luann shoots Dorothy a look.

I know I just needed to calm down it's all I have, she tells Luann what Paul said when she suggested separation about leaving her forever.

Luann is angry, she always thought Paul was bossy and controlling when she pulled Paul aside and told him he treats Dorothy like a horse.

He shot back and said *well that keeps her in line.*

Dorothy believes Paul found her and nurtured her, that she owes him, but Luann views it differently.

It doesn't take a rocket scientist to see that Paul is a ticking time bomb.

****

Hugh Hefner sits at a table surrounded by playmates and dozens of photographers.

It's nothing unusual for Mr. Playboy, but today is different.

Today, he's announcing the 1980 Playmate of the Year.

It's a lunchtime event, and big round tables have been set out on Playboy's great lawn.

The videographer is on hand to document everything.

As people settle into their seats, Hef takes the stage.

There's a hush as he begins to speak:

"It's a very real pleasure to be here and a pleasure to welcome all of you here for the presentation of our 1980 Playmate of the Year and she is something rather special. They always are, but Dorothy is unique and now it gives me a great deal of pleasure to announce her and introduce her as our 1980 Playmate of the Year Canadian-born Dorothy Stratten. Dorothy wanna come up here?".

The camera shows Dorothy with a spotlight, seated on a chair, taking their nervous breath.

But when she gets on stage, she looks completely poised in her gold strapless dress and bright blonde hair.

Hef hands are a cheque for $25,000 and a special gold plaque of her issues covered.

It's all part of a prize package of over $200,000.

Hef says, *to you, Dorothy with a great deal of love,* and he means it.

Dorothy mouths the word, Thank you and leans for a quick kiss.

Minutes after she steps up to the microphone she says, *"I'm sure that this has been many a girl's dream, and certainly many of the Playmate's dream, and it's been mine. I would like to thank my other half, my photographer, Mario Casselli, who I've practically had under contract for the last year and a half.*

And Marilyn Grabowski and Elizabeth Norris and Mickey Garcia, who have helped me and also become my best friends, and Hef, who has made me probably the happiest girl in the world today, thank you".

Hef stands up to the side watching Dorothy Shine, to think Almost a year ago she was almost too shy to speak.

THE MURDER OF A STARLET

Not one of his playmates has come so far, so fast, or sparkles quite the way, Dorothy does.

It amazes him how humble she still is even now.

She's on her way to becoming a star and he couldn't be prouder.

In her promotional tours, she even handles difficult questions with honesty and poise.

Surrounded as you are in the entertainment magazine business by so many con men, isn't it awfully hard to live a normal life now? A reporter asks her.

Well, what is a normal life? Dorothy says

Dorothy's trajectory to fame has been anything but normal.

As Hef scans the crowd, he briefly locks eyes with Paul.

He's holding a drink, his expression morose, even with that fake smile plastered on his face.

But his eyes are shifty, resentful like he's not sure why it's not him standing in the spotlight with Dorothy.

Hef is glad he had the staff put Paul at another table.

He doesn't want the guy ruining Dorothy's afternoon.

Dorothy is overflowing with gratitude, she still can't believe all this attention is for her and the kind words from Hef nearly made her cry.

After the ceremony, she sits down with Elizabeth Norris and pages through a photo album filled with her photos from Playboy shoots.

Elizabeth has become more than a handler and PR companion, she's a friend.

When they go through the book reminiscing together, cameramen snap photos and tell Dorothy to look their way.

Paul slides into the chair on her left, she's hardly seen him all afternoon, just a glimpse behind a photographer earlier in the day.

The truth is, she's been avoiding him, it's hard for her to concentrate when he's around.

He grabbed her hand and said to her, *look at all this, huh? we did it.*

She smiles at him politely and squeezes his hand back, and then she turns back to the photos and lets his hand drop under the table.

She doesn't even like touching him anymore.

He leans in I'm hungry, you want something to eat? He asks with that smile, always that smile, like he's trying to impress people who aren't even looking.

She used to find it endearing now she wishes he would just go away.

But he won't, he asks again, louder, you want something to eat?

She keeps her eyes averted and shakes her head.

No, God, she hopes he doesn't make a scene, not today.

When he heads to the bar, one of the PR ladies comes over to Dorothy.

Are you OK?

No, she says with more vehemence than she expected, but she shakes it off. She still has a Carson appearance to do.

THE MURDER OF A STARLET

****

Johnny Carson has been taping the Tonight Show every afternoon for more than 15 years.

Any celebrity with a movie album or book to promote stops by and why wouldn't they? Viewership is in the millions.

Carson's known for his playful attitude and perfect pauses, but under his laid-back to meaner, he's tough.

He only laughs when something is funny and when a guest is boring or monotonous, he surprises his producers by announcing a commercial break.

In other words, he brooks no fools and everyone knows it.

Robert Blake once likened talking to Carson to facing off against a firing squad, but guests keep coming back because the publicity is priceless.

On April 30th, the main guest was actor Charlton Heston.

THE MURDER OF A STARLET

Dorothy Spot comes midway through the show following a comedian.

She waits nervously backstage for her cue and listens to the audience murmurs from the other side of the curtain.

She thinks about how many times she's watched the show from home, she can't believe she's here.

And then she hears the familiar voice.

About a year ago, my next guest was working at an ice cream stand in Vancouver and her boyfriend talked during the sending of some photographs, which he sent off to Playboy magazine, and this is the result. Yesterday she was named Playmates of the Year. Oh, we thought, we would say the dessert to last for sure right, Welcome Dorothy Stratten?

Dorothy walks out in a white gown and hugs her curves, but not too much, the neckline is hot.

There's an innocence about her look enhanced by the flower in her hair.

She looks poised like a budding young actress more than a Playboy sex kitten.

When she sits down Carson holds up the June issue, he says *the high golly, it's you.*

Then he jumps right in and asks her about how Playboy found her and what prizes she won for being Playmate of the Year.

Dorothy lights up and says,

I got a $65,000 Russian sable fur coat and a $25,000 cheque a $26,000 Jaguar and a $13,000 bathtub. The 13,100%, it's made of brass and it was handmade and it has four jacuzzi jets on the inside. It fits about 10 people.

They are only a couple of minutes into the interview, but she already has the audience eating out of her hand.

Johnny is gentle with his questions and sometimes just a little flirtatious.

He knows she's nervous, but as Dorothy warms up, she surprises Carson, which doesn't happen very often. Both Johnny and his studio audience are completely charmed.

There will be no early commercial breaks tonight.

THE MURDER OF A STARLET

****

Dorothy sits at the small lacquered desk, staring out at the Montreal skyline.

She's never written a letter like this, but it's time.

After Dorothy's Carson appearance, she hopped on a plane for a two-week promotional tour and Paul's calls have dogged her from city to city.

And when they talk, he's always angry.

More nights than not, she cries herself to sleep.

She knows her feelings have changed.

She just needs space to clear her head without him badgering her and trying to make her feel guilty.

Dear Paul, she writes, she's not sure what to say next, she scribbles a few lines, then tears up the paper and starts over again.

She continues to write again, It's hard to find the right words, so she closes her eyes and channels her feelings like she used to do when she wrote in her diary back in high school.

God, it feels like a lifetime ago, back when she could never imagine all this.

Back when Paul used to say they were going to the moon and they would be together forever now, she felt suffocated.

So that's what she writes, *I need some time to be me,* "*I feel manipulated, controlled and smothered. I just want to be my person*".

Then she remembers us saying she read somewhere the picture in her mind of a bird in a cage.

She writes "*Let the bird fly If you love me, you'll let me go. If what we had was right, I'll come back*".

When she's done, Dorothy puts the letter in an envelope and sends it off by Courier to Paul.

Then she waits.

A few nights later, she's fast asleep when the phone rings, it's Paul.

He's yelling and ranting and raving.

She doesn't even know what he's saying, he makes her feel so small.

THE MURDER OF A STARLET

Let the bird fly? what the hell does that mean?

Paul sits on the couch and has W Clarkson's apartment, the letter in his lap he's read it 100 times, but it still doesn't make sense.

Hello...(silence) did she hang up? then he hears her voice.

Oh, hi.

Ohh hi? H asks (more silence).

Her voice is soft.

The letter means what it says, Paul, I want to be free and if we're supposed to be together, we will.

Paul's heart is racing, supposed to be, I'm your fucking husband, you think you can just write me a letter and I'll go away just like that? After everything I've done for you?

Dorothy says she just needs some time to think.

It's not your fault Paul, it's me, she says. I'm not trying to hurt you.

His voice takes on a wheedling tone, what about me? what am I supposed to do now? Paul asks.

You are supposed to be free too, she says.

Then the line goes dead.

Paul stares at the phone he's not giving up, there's too much at stake.

A few days later, he calls again, this time he's calm.

I just want to let you know I'll be in Vancouver, he says. I'm coming to your mother's wedding, I'm part of the family too.

Dorothy doesn't have it in her to fight.

OK, she says you can come.

THE WEDDING

Dorothy makes her way through the crowd, clutching 3 very full glasses of champagne.

She tries not to spill anything as she hands the drinks to a group of women standing next to a buffet table.

It's May 10th and Dorothy is in Vancouver at her mother's house, it's a low-key wedding reception, just family and friends.

THE MURDER OF A STARLET

It's good to be home and see her brother and sister again.

She can't believe how fast Louise has grown, she's 12 now, and John is 19 already a young man.

Playboy arranged for Vancouver to be the last stop on Dorothy's tour so she could attend the wedding.

Dorothy likes Nellie's new husband, Burl.

He's a soft-spoken mechanic who restores old cars he and Nellie only dated for a month before he popped the question, but clearly, he's crazy about her mom.

A woman Dorothy's never met shyly approaches, *Can you take a photo with us?* she asks and points to her husband.

Of course, Dorothy says, squeezing in between the couple and smiling wide for the camera.

Everyone's been clamoring for pictures with her ever since she arrived.

They're calling her their hometown girl turned celebrity.

She's delighted to play the part; it helps her forget she's in a troubled marriage.

She wishes she never agreed to let Paul come, but it's too late now.

Let's get this party started, Paul Schneider thumbs the palm of his hand on the top of the bar and shoots a smile at Dorothy's brother.

How's it going, kid? he didn't wait for an answer and said Pour me some of that cognac, and don't be shy.

Paul scans the crowd of local yokel types, he thinks, he is not surprised, It's not like Nelly married up.

Dorothy would have ended up just like her mother if he hadn't stepped in and changed her future.

And lately, he's getting tired of reminding her.

He watches Dorothy pose for photos and then she signs her name on a cocktail napkin for some old guy in a brown polyester suit, even giving him a little Peck on the cheek.

When the guy walks away, Paul grabs her hand and leads her into a corner.

I should have set up a booth and charged everyone to take a picture with you.

THE MURDER OF A STARLET

Dorothy gently takes her hand out of his, let's talk later, she says, today about my mom, not me.

Fine, Paul thinks.

It's not like he flew to Vancouver for any grand romantic gestures.

He's here to talk sense into her and make some money on the side.

This town is still his turf, there are plenty of clubs who would jump at the chance to book an appearance with the playboy of the year.

Paul heads over to the kitchen and starts making some calls.

Hey, it's Paul Snider, You've *got an opportunity, Dorothy Stratten is in town.*

Of course, everyone's only too happy to oblige.

After just a few calls, he's got Dorothy booked solid for the next several days, and he'll pocket the money, feels good to be back.

It's time to get the hell out of here.

THE MURDER OF A STARLET

Dorothy's not quite sure why she lets Paul come back to her hotel suite with her, but she does.

As soon as they're in the room, it's the same argument again.

He tells her she owes him, she needs to stay in Canada and do some nightclub dates.

It's the least she can do.

And then he's on to the letter, what does she mean about feeling caged? He's the one who set her free.

Then he threatens her, he tells her he'll leave her go to Hawaii, and never speak to her again.

When he goes downstairs to take a dip in the pool.

She calls her mom, she says he was so mean, Mom.

Then she calls Peter and tells him what Paul said about leaving.

Good let him go, Peter says. B

ut Dorothy's scared *I don't want him to go off upset*, she tells him.

She still thinks they can be friends.

THE MURDER OF A STARLET

Paul's why I'm here.

She hears a note of impatience in Peter's voice. That's ridiculous, he says.

Is it? If I hadn't done Playboy, I wouldn't have met you.

Peter's quiet.

Isn't that true?

finally, Peter says you don't owe him your life Dorothy, you've worked hard to get where you are, he's a sponge.

Dorothy hears the keys in the door, Paul is back.

I have to go, she says.

For the next few days, Dorothy follows Paul from club to club.

He brags to anyone who will listen about all his accomplishments in Hollywood.

She signs a few autographs and poses for pictures, and then Paul collects the cash and moves her on to the next place.

THE MURDER OF A STARLET

Dorothy hopes by going along with it, he'll leave her alone. Then she can get back to Peter and New York.

She'll figure out what to do then.

****

Peter Bogdanovich is relieved when Dorothy arrives in New York in the third week of May.

He tells her he is worried that she has changed her mind about their relationship.

Dorothy cries and assures him she still feels the same, but she's not sure what to do about Paul.

Peter softens he hates to see her cry.

They'll have the next few weeks together to finish shooting the film and talk this through. When they're shooting, Peter's intuition about Dorothy proves true.

She has a natural sense of comic timing, there's nuance to the way she performs.

It's like she becomes the character.

When she's not in a shot, she sits quietly reading.

She goes through several books of poetry and classic novels and asks Peter's advice about what to read next.

She reads Dickens and Hemingway and tells him her favorite is Dostoyevsky. She loves the way he writes about people, the good and the bad.

Everybody who sees the rushes from the D.P. to the editor is bowled over by her beauty.

But even more than that, her skill.

When Dorothy's in a shot, you can't look away.

There's no doubt in Peters's mind Dorothy is going to be a star.

For Dorothy, Life is exhilarating.

If she's not shooting scenes, she's back at her hotel room on calls with her business manager and agent.

Vogue and Harpers Bazaar have expressed interest in putting her on the cover when the movie is released.

No playmate has ever been on the cover of a major fashion magazine after posing nude.

There are also inquiries for TV roles and more movies.

It's overwhelming. Dorothy's just 20 years old and it's all happening so fast.

She calls Hef for advice.

How is this done?

Hef is reassuring, he tells her when she's back in LA He will help her sort it out.

Peters is a God sent to advise his support.

She finds herself spending more and more nights in his hotel suite.

When she's in her room, she instructs the front desk to take a message whenever Paul calls.

She's still not sure what to do about the marriage, but she's getting closer to making a decision.

One in rainy morning in June, she writes her mom and Birla a letter.

Nelly's been worried since she last saw Dorothy in Vancouver with Paul.

Both she and Beryl are certain that Paul is exploiting Dorothy's kindness, and if they separate, he will find a way to take advantage of her financially.

Dorothy writes:

"Thank you very much for all your concern and advice, but as you know, my problem goes much deeper than money.

And as you also know, I don't intend to use money as an excuse, everyone needs money to live but I won't decide about my marriage on that basis. All I want is to be happy, no matter how rich or poor. And if it makes me happy to give everything away for my freedom, then that's what I'll do".

Dorothy means it, she may have promised Paul half of everything, but she never promised him her freedom.

At the end of June, she talked to her business manager and then a lawyer Peter recommended, Wayne Alexander.

She tells him she doesn't want to hurt Paul, but she wants to make a clean break.

The lawyer tells her all she needs to do legally is write Paul a letter stating she intends to get a separate residence when she returns to LA.

By the end of June, Dorothy comes to a decision.

She sends Paul a letter declaring she wants a physical and financial separation.

****

For the last three weeks, Paul's been on Edge, ever since he got back from Vancouver.

He got Dorothy to come around when he threatened to leave, but now she's in New York and he can't reach her.

Every time he calls to get some stupid receptionist at the front desk or says Dorothy asked not to be disturbed.

When he leaves messages that her husband called she rarely calls back.

When he does reach her, they fight.

More often than not, she hangs up saying she has to go memorize lines.

THE MURDER OF A STARLET

He tries to get his mind off her by going to the mansion, but they won't let him in without Dorothy.

Where's the gratitude? without him, Playboy wouldn't have a playmate of the year.

He starts hitting the clubs, hanging on his card, and looking for girls he can mold and shape into playmates and stars.

Sometimes he goes over to his buddy Chips.

He met him through Dorothy last year.

Chip's girlfriend Luann is Miss June.

He doesn't like Luann much, She's hot, but sometimes she sticks her nose where it doesn't belong.

But Chips is a cool guy, a laidback surfer type who manages a health club.

On other days, Paul brings a girl with him.

They're usually the same type, young, sympathetic, and nurturing.

THE MURDER OF A STARLET

Inevitably, he finds himself whining about Dorothy while they console him, which puts him back on edge.

Why won't she take his calls?

Then one afternoon in late June, he's sitting on his couch watching reruns of Hogans Heroes when his roommate Steve drops a letter into his lap.

It's got a green tag attached that says certified.

The return address is a lawyer named Wayne Alexander. He has no idea who it is.

He tears it open and starts to read, it's a letter from Dorothy, but he doesn't understand.

She says when she gets home, she's going to get her place, she wants a separation.

His stomach drops, is she kidding? he slumps back on the couch.

This can be her, the Dorothy he knows would never do this to him.

He thinks somebody's pulling her strings.

She's been different ever since she started shooting the movie in New York.

When he thinks it through, he starts connecting the dots.

Bogdonavich, the big-time Hollywood director, he's probably behind this whole thing.

Paul Springs is in action, at first he heads down to the bank and cleans out their joint account.

It's only 1500 bucks, but it's enough for some retail therapy.

He buys himself some new clothes, a pair of boots, and a Cobra skin belt.

Uses the rest to install the stereo equipment in the living room where Dorothy won his Playmate of the Year.

Next, he finds a family law attorney Michael Kelly reps actors and actresses and messy custody and divorce battles.

Paul wants to make sure if Dorothy goes through with this, he gets everything.

He tells the lawyer he suspects Dorothy's having an affair with her director, and now he's gotten in her head.

Can he sue him for breaching the management contract?

Kelly tells him he can't do anything without proof.

How do I get that? he asks,

Kelly digs a business card out of a drawer and slices it across his desk.

Paul picks it up and reads, Mark L. Goldstein, private investigator.

CHAPTER 6.

Last Days

Paul Snider sits at a table in a Brentwood coffee shop, drumming his fingers.

It's mid-morning the first week in July 1980 and there's not a cloud in the clear blue sky.

If only the same could be said for Paul's mood.

His marriage to Dorothy Stratten is in shambles, she wants a separation.

She didn't even tell him in person, she just sent papers through the mail via some lawyer.

Paul's been trying to call her, but the hotel in New York says she's checked out.

He's sure Peter Bogdanovich has something to do with this.

Mr Schneider, a small man stands over his table, holding out his hand.

I'm Mark Goldstein, the private investigator.

THE MURDER OF A STARLET

What can I do for you?

Paul motions to the booth across from him and it gets right to the point and said I need you to help me build a case, I think my wife might be having an affair with her director, but I need proof.

Goldstein notes, that he's just 26 years old, but he knows the law and how to exploit it to a client's advantage.

Before he became a private detective, he'd gone to law school and started practicing before he even graduated.

His specialty was litigation, he loved to sue and went after companies big and small telephone companies Macy's, and Whirlpool washers even sued his uncle for fraud.

One defendant testified Goldstein threatened to have him killed.

When the California bar caught wind of his Rep, they refused him admission for moral disqualification.

So Goldstein reinvented himself as a private detective.

His legal background helps him get whatever it takes to make a case.

Paul and Goldstein hit it off right away.

Paul tells him he's not only the aggrieved husband, he's Dorothy's manager, and they have a deal 50/50 split for all her earnings.

He thinks Bogdanovich is behind Dorothy's decision to leave him and he wants to sue.

Bogdanovich probably has millions, the least he can do is give some to Paul to help ease the pain of losing his wife.

Goldstein tells him he's happy to help.

Do you guys still have a joint account? he asks.

Paul tells him they do, but he's cleaning that out.

The bulk of her money is in her company, Stratten Enterprises, and he's not an officer.

I'm going to straighten this out ASAP, Paul tells him. I'm going to talk to Bob Houston, he's the business manager.

But when he gets to Houston's office, it doesn't go how he hoped.

Houston tells him. Dorothy has offered to pay all of Paul's bills, plus the cash settlement and half of everything Dorothy has earned to date.

How much does that come out to, Bob?

It's about $40,000 after taxes, plenty of money to start over. It's more than fair.

Paul doesn't think it's fair at all.

The agreement was 50/50.

That doesn't work for me Bob, I want alimony specifically 50% for the next three years.

Heuston doesn't burg and asks, haven't you taken enough from this woman already? This extortion is over.

But for Paul, this isn't over at all, equal partners, he said, and he won't settle for less than his fair share.

Dorothy has been doing her best to keep her relationship with Peter a secret, not even Playboy or Heffner know, and the press doesn't pick up on it either.

Filming is almost over and the two have plans to take a vacation together to London.

Dorothy has only been overseas once when she was four.

Peter promises to take her to the theatre and museums.

She's never been to a museum before.

She even manages to put Paul out of her mind, at least most of the time.

Dorothy just hopes he's coming to terms with everything and can start a new life with her settlement offer.

Move on and do something on his own, but he hasn't.

The day after shooting wraps, there's a knock on the door.

Dorothy is still in her pajamas, there was a cast party the night before that went late, and she and Peter decided to sleep in.

When she opens the door, she's surprised to see Bill and Susan Latrasse standing outside holding a Manila envelope in their hands.

Paul commissioned them last year to take photos of Dorothy for a poster he thought could sell millions.

But she recently told Paul she had changed her mind.

How did they know where to find her? I'm sorry, but I can't invite you in, other people are here.

Bill holds up the folder.

It's OK we just want you to look at the photos. We're hoping you'll reconsider the project; we've put a lot of work into this.

Dorothy's confused is Paul behind this?

But she's too afraid to ask.

She quickly flips through the proofs, shots of her in black and sitting under disco lights wearing a sparkly red bodysuit and a tuxedo bow,

It seems so long ago.

Give me a minute, she says and slips back inside.

She finds Peter pacing in the bedroom.

It's the photographers who took those roller skating pictures, she tells him.

THE MURDER OF A STARLET

They flew all the way here from LA.

Peter looks over her shoulder at the shots, Dorothy can see he doesn't like them.

They make you look ordinary, he says, but it's up to her.

Dorothy looks at the photos again Peter's right, but she hates letting people down.

When she returns, she tells the Liechassis. She's confused.

Did you show these to Paul? She asks.

We need your permission Bill says, since you're divorcing Paul.

Dorothy hesitates and then hands the photos back and tells him she's sorry, but the answer is no.

****

It's a sunny day in the middle of July, and Paul Schneider is in a dark place, his mood swinging between despair and anger.

THE MURDER OF A STARLET

The roller skating poster deal appears to be dead, he blames Bogdanovich.

He's got Goldstein trying to dig up information on the director.

Paul still needs proof that Bogdanovich is influencing Dorothy.

And then he finds something that hits him hard.

While rummaging through Dorothy's things, he comes across poems and love letters to Dorothy from Peter.

Are they having an affair? What else is she holding back?

Find out if Dorothy has any assets I don't know about, he tells Goldstein. I'm entitled to half to see what you can find out about Peter Bogdanovich.

But as the days go by, Paul starts losing hope.

How can he ever take on a Goliath like Peter Bogdanovich?

Paul doesn't have half his money or power.

Bogdanovich is a major director, not to mention that he is Hef's good friend.

He tells a friend despairingly, maybe this thing is too big for me.

He feels his options falling away.

I suppose I could go back to Vancouver, he tells a friend.

But he knows he'll never do that again.

Everyone will smell the failure on him.

One night, he calls photographer Bill Retrosi sobbing.

He tells him he's afraid he won't ever see Dorothy again, *I can't get near her, she's surrounded by attorneys, she won't even take my calls.*

He decides if he can't reach her by phone, he'll try and appeal in the mail, but he's not exactly sure what to write.

I can't get it together without you, he scribbles and then he's not sure what else to say.

THE MURDER OF A STARLET

He draughts a letter to Bogdanovich telling him if he stops influencing Dorothy, Paul will forgive him.

But he doesn't send that one either.

He finally settles on a photo album of all the greeting cards he gave her since they met, he wraps it up and sends it to her hotel in New York.

When she doesn't respond, he sends a self-help book explaining what men need.

He feels like he's falling apart.

One night, when his roommate Steve Kushner comes home, he finds Paul sitting in the dark, staring into the void.

Damn, man, are you OK? Steve asks.

This is hard, Paul says and starts to sob.

But Kushner doesn't understand, nobody does.

Paul finds cold comfort in a 38 revolver he borrowed a few months back from his friend.

For protection, he told him.

THE MURDER OF A STARLET

Now Paul sits on his bed and spends the cylinder around and around, wondering what it would feel like to pull the trigger.

****

When Dorothy steps onto the conquered jet with Peter, it feels like a dream.

She'd never flown on a plane so luxurious or so fast, just three and a half hours from New York to London.

For gourmet meals, every seed is first class.

Peter's taken every precaution for their trip to be a secret.

They check into the hotel under assumed names and then over the next 10 days he shows Dorothy the town and takes her to restaurants museums and plays.

It feels like a clandestine honeymoon, a hint of what the future will be like with Peter by her side.

The trip is almost perfect, except for the feeling she's left something unfinished behind, something not right.

When their trip is over and they get to JFK, Dorothy is slammed back to reality.

Customs officials tell her that her work visa has expired.

She's confused, Playboy immigration lawyers told her this was handled.

She sees Peter step forward with an angry look on his face.

She held up her hand and *said I'll make a call and get this all straightened out.*

When she gets to the pay phone, she realizes she doesn't have enough change, so she decides to charge it to the West Clarkson address.

It means the operator will have to ring the house, Dorothy praised their roommate Steve Kushner will answer the phone, but he doesn't, it's Paul.

Now he knows she's back in the states trying to return to LA, it makes her uneasy.

THE MURDER OF A STARLET

On the flight home, she grabs Peter's arm and starts to cry.

I'm scared, she says, but I don't know why.

The first call Paul makes when he gets off the phone is to Goldstein, *Dorothy's coming home,* he tells the investigator to check all inbound flights from New York and if you miss her stakeout, Bogdanovich's house,

I want to know where she is.

A young blonde woman pokes her head in the door, everything OK?

Paul met Patty Lauerman at an auto show last year.

She was 17 years old, a checkout girl from Riverside who did small-time modeling on the side.

She's leggy and blonde, just like Dorothy.

He sees Playmate's potential, so he starts to groom her.

He teaches her to walk like Dorothy dress like Dorothy and wear her hair like Dorothy.

And then he moves her in thinking maybe lightning can strike twice.

He smiles at her now, everything's fine just talking to Goldstein, but everything is not fine Dorothy isn't here.

He remembers that the biggest Playboy event of the year is coming up Hefner's Midsummer Night's Dream Party. He figured he and Dorothy would go together. Now he tortures himself, thinking about her showing up on Bogdanovich's arm.

He calls the mansion, who gets an invite and brings Patty, making her jealous.

But the receptionist tells him he's not on the list.

Well, then put me on the list, tell Hef it's Paul, Paul Schneider, Dorothy Stratten's husband,

Sorry, she says.

When Goldstein comes by, Paul complains.

I've been banned from the mansion unless I'm with Dorothy.

But Goldstein has news of his own.

THE MURDER OF A STARLET

He's found out Dorothy has a new address in Beverly Hills.

Only that she doesn't live there, she's moved in with Peter Bogdanovich.

****

Paul Schneider sits in the bushes staring at the gate, a 38 Special clutched to his chest.

Behind the gate is Peter Bogdanovich's house, and he's waiting for Dorothy or Bogdanovich to come out.

He parked down the street across Sunset Blvd and walked the two blocks.

He remembers the house from the time he drove Dorothy here to audition.

Bogdanovich probably hit on her back then, too.

He's been here for hours and nothing has moved except an occasional passing car, so he's had a lot of time to think.

He's not sure what he'll do if he sees them, maybe he'll threaten to shoot himself unless Dorothy talks to him or maybe he can reason with Bogdanovich, give Dorothy back and there will be no hard feelings.

Finally, he gets tired of waiting.

He jogs back to the car under the waning moon, but he's not ready to go home, his brain is spinning out.

He speeds through the twists and turns of Mulholland Drive to a hill overlooking the twinkling lights of the Bel Air mansions.

He imagines all the smug people and their smug homes sipping martinis.

He wishes he was one of those people.

He thinks about killing himself.

He pulls out the gun and holds it to his head.

His finger pours on the trigger, he closes his eyes, feeling the pressure and then..... he can't.

He jumps out of the car and angrily shoots into the air once, twice, the sound echoes down the canyons.

Then he gets back into his car and drives home.

There has to be another way, he thinks.

THE MURDER OF A STARLET

****

It's Monday, August 4th, 1987, o'clock in the evening at the Astrodome in Houston, TX.

The Astros are set to square off against the San Francisco Giants, and Dorothy is in town to throw out tonight's first pitch.

It's been a red-hot season for the team and the ballpark is packed with yet another sellout crowd.

Dorothy runs out in white pants and sneakers.

She carries a baseball glove in her hand.

The catcher trots over to the mound amid good-natured catcalls and whistles.

He hands Dorothy the baseball, and she lifts it into the air and tosses the ball back to him, the official first pitch and the crowd goes wild.

Her appearance is part of the Playmate of the Year promotional tour.

This trip, she'll only be gone a few days and she's glad.

She can't wait to get home to Peter.

His place feels like home; she adores his daughters, and they remind her of her sister Louise. The only thing hanging over her head is Paul. She still thinks about him sometimes she feels guilty about hurting him.

Some nights when she gets back to her room, she cries.

What if he hurts himself? Maybe if she just talks to him, she can reassure him that they can still be friends.

Hi, Dorothy says in a whisper, it's me.

At first, all Dorothy can hear is the sound of him breathing, but then she thinks she hears a sob.

I miss you, why won't you come home? Paul asks.

we talked about this, Paul, remember I need to move on.

Well, what about me, Dorothy? I'm broke. Don't you even care about that?

Of course, I care, she sighs.

THE MURDER OF A STARLET

Then why are you with that director? I can't even get a hold of you anymore.

Dorothy tells him she's trying to talk to him now.

He goes silent for a minute, then he says If you care to meet me in person, let's have lunch.

Dorothy thinks for a moment, what harm is one lunch and maybe she can get this whole thing straightened out.

Sure, she said, how about Friday? She asks, she can sense Paul's mood lift. Friday, August 8th It's a date.

****

It's August 7th and Paul feels like he's back, he's finally going to see Dorothy in person. It'll be different this time; he tells a couple of friends at dinner.

I'll let her know I've changed, it's going to be him and Dorothy from now on. Just like the old days.

And if she doesn't want to see it his way, he's got a back-pocket plan.

Goldstein found some information on Peter Bogdanovich, things he plans to share with Dorothy.

She needs to know it's Paul who has her best interests at heart, but he doesn't anticipate needing to play that card.

He's back on top, the Queen is coming back, he shouts.

The next morning, Paul wakes up and puts on a three-piece tan suit, the same one he wore at their wedding.

He instructs Patty to clean the house from top to bottom.

He buys champagne and roses and sets them on the dining room table, and then he waits.

Dorothy pulls up to Paul's house on West Clarkson Road and throws the cougar in Park.

It's August 8th and it's the first time she's been here in over two months.

She doesn't want to be back, but she still feels she owes Paul.

At the front door, she hesitates, should she let herself in or knock? But then the door swings open and there's Paul with a big goofy grin holding a bouquet of roses in his hand.

THE MURDER OF A STARLET

She notices he's wearing the suit he wore on their wedding day.

She looks down at her casual clothes, Paul sees it, too, and his face falls.

You didn't dress up, he asks.

We're just having lunch Dorothy says.

Paul quickly resets his smile, we've got time Come in. I've got a surprise, he steps aside.

The place is cleaner than Dorothy, remembers it, even the shades are up.

On the table is a bottle of champagne with a card just like Paul to go for the big gestures.

But Dorothy isn't that girl anymore.

Let's go eat, she says, we need to talk.

Lunch is a disaster, the place is packed and it's hard to hear over the noise that she tries, she tells Paul gently that she is serious about the letter and she wants a separation.

She wants to settle the finances as well, but it will be fair.

She has no intention of leaving him out.

Paul isn't happy about this at all, they ride back to the house in silence.

When they get back to the house, he tells her he wants her to come home.

I've changed, Dorothy, really why can't we try again?

Dorothy crosses her arms and says I can't, Paul It's too late.

Paul bristles you can't or you won't.

I'm in love with Peter, she can't believe she said it, but she's glad she did.

At least now it's in the open.

Paul jumps up and starts to pace.

He's using you, Dorothy, and I can prove it.

I've been looking into your director, he destroyed Civil Shepherd's career, is that how you want to end up?

Dorothy tells Paul to stop, but his voice gets loud.

Peter paid a girl $5000 to have sex with him and another guy in the grotto at the mansion, he says, that's the kind of guy you're in love with?

Dorothy shakes her head saying she doesn't believe that.

But Paul keeps pushing, maybe that's the kind of sex you're into, huh, Dorothy?

His voice gets so loud Steve Kushner's dog starts to bark.

Steve hears it too, he pads down the stairs pokes in his head, and asks, everything OK?

Paul took a breath and answered, it's fine just talking

It's like a reset.

When Steve's gone, Paul sinks into the couch and starts to cry.

You're being brainwashed, he tells her.

Dorothy cries too, look, Paul, we can still be friends. We'll always be friends.

When Patty gets home, Dorothy is relieved to see her, she wants Paul to be happy.

Before she leaves, Dorothy goes through her things. All the clothes she wore just a few months ago now feel like they belong to someone else.

She takes one or two pieces and tells Paul to give the rest to Patty.

Then she tells him she has to go, *I'll call you on Sunday to check in,* she promises.

When Dorothy leaves, Patty asks Paul how it went. *I couldn't get through to her, nothing I say sinks in anymore. Bogdanovich has her in the palm of his hand,* Paul says.

Later that evening, Paul is watching TV with Mark Goldstein and Patty when he hears the knock on the front door, he knows what's coming.

Chip and Luann are here to get the gun back. Chip is moving to Florida and he wants to make sure Luann keeps the 38 for protection.

Paul's going to miss the guy.

They were working on, one of Paul's ideas building weight benches for clients and health clubs Chip managed.

THE MURDER OF A STARLET

They're gonna sell them through ads in the local paper.

Paul even thought of expanding the idea into sex benches, he thinks they can sell them to sex shops.

He has one sitting in his room, but with Chip leaving the project is fizzling out.

Paul walks over to a drawer to retrieve the gun to get back to Chip.

Give me a minute, he says, and then he walks outside and looks at the night sky.

A permanent glow from L.A's lights makes it impossible to see any stars.

He lifts the gun, corks the trigger, and shoots once.

Then he lets out a shrill laugh, he hears Chip yelling.

Are you? shooting the gun.

Don't worry, that was just a backfire on the ten, he shouts back.

Later Chip checks the cylinder and discovers three shots have been fired.

He asked Paul what happened.

Paul tells him the truth, I sat in my car the other night and thought about straining things out of my way.

Chip looks large.

Paul tells him, it's a sobering experience to sit there and contemplate in the end.

It's not the first time Paul has shared his thoughts about death, he told the girl he was dating he thought about killing Dorothy and then turning the gun on himself. Then that would be a Hollywood ending.

****

Dorothy feels like her happily ever after is just around the corner.

It's August 9th and her little sister Louise is in town and they're staying with Peter.

On Sunday, a chauffeur picks up Dorothy and Louise and drives them out to the Mojave Desert.

It's a shoot for a sunglasses company owned by Playboy.

By the time they settle in, it's late and Dorothy realizes she forgot to call Paul, she'll phone him tomorrow.

The next day, she reaches him at lunch.

I'm sorry, she says Louise is in town, it's been a bit crazy, are you OK? She asks.

You say you want to be friends and now you can't even remember to call and no, I'm not OK, he tells her he needs cash.

She can feel him getting worked up.

I almost blew my brains out Dorothy, that's the kind of stress you're causing me, after all, I've done for you.

I'm sorry Paul, Dorothy says.

It feels familiar, Why is she always apologizing to him?

Paul asks her to come by Thursday to work out the financial details of the split.

Dorothy's not sure she wants to see him in person again, but she still feels guilty.

OK, she says I have a meeting with Houston in the morning, I'll come by after that.

When she hangs up, she decides not to tell anyone, they wouldn't understand.

It's Tuesday, August 12th, early evening at the Playboy Mansion in Bel Air things are quiet except for the sound of crickets and an occasional call from a Peacock to his mate.

Inside the mansion living room, Hugh Hefner sits on a low back couch, watching Peter Bogdanovich pace back and forth.

Hef hasn't talked to Peter since his film wrapped in July and Peter is excited to share how well it all went, especially Dorothy's performance.

She was just marvelous Hef, Peter says, You're gonna be so proud of her.

Hef nods.

He already is.

Then Peter's face takes on a different look, more serious, almost contemplative.

I have something to tell you, he says,

Dorothy and I are involved, we're in a relationship.

Hef is surprised, sure he's heard rumors, but he never puts much stock in that.

He jokes saying, I didn't know you were so good at keeping secrets.

Peter explains they wanted to keep it all low profile until the movie comes out and until things are settled with Paul.

I hope this isn't just a casual fling Peter, Hef says.

Peter shakes his head and says to Hef, am in love Hef really in love I've never felt this way about anyone in my life.

Wednesday, August 13th is a damn fine day for Paul Schneider.

He practically struts into Bill and Susan's literary photography studio armed with a lopsided grin.

He's here to look over patties and new modeling photos that the couple recently shot.

As he examines the proof, he points to a few shots and Patty in a bikini pouting for the camera.

These look pretty good, he says.

He shuffles through a few more photos and says, she looks a little like playmate Claudia Jennings, don't you think? You know the girl who died in that car accident last year?

And Paul says, you know, sometimes a playmate dies, and sometimes actresses die before their movie comes out.

When that happens causes a lot of trouble. His face lit up and he said hey, guess what I did today? I went by myself a gun, a Legit rifle.

The gun purchases are what put him in such high spirits.

Since Chip had taken back the 38 last Friday, he had been trying to buy a replacement first gun store, but the sales clerk wouldn't sell him one, giving some bullshit reason about Paul being a Canadian citizen.

Then there was a guy selling a 12-gauge Mossberg pump shotgun through some local paper called the Recycler.

Wasn't asking any questions, Paul scored it for 125 bucks.

Why on Earth would you need a gun? he asks.

THE MURDER OF A STARLET

I'm gonna take up hunting, he winks.

As soon as Paul gets home, he pulls a shotgun out of his closet, aims it, looks through the barrel a couple of times, and then picks up the phone to call a writer he knows.

A few months ago, he gave me 1000 bucks as a down payment to write a biography about him.

When the guy answers, Paul says, hang on to my story it's gonna be worth something, then he hangs up.

On Thursday, August 14th, Dorothy woke up early.

 She hasn't been sleeping well lately, and today she feels jittery.

She's meeting Paul later, and she knows Peter won't approve.

She hates lying to him, but she's worried about Paul hurting himself. She'll tell Peter everything later, once this is done.

The only person she tells her sister, Louise, she makes her promise not to tell anyone. She even asks her if she wants to come along, but Louise says she'd rather stay back and play with Peters's daughters.

Dorothy hugs her close and says she's going to the office of her business manager first, then Paul's.

It shouldn't take long Dorothy says I'll be back before 2:30.

Promise? Louise says.

Dorothy looked into her eyes and replied to her, *I promise.*

When Paul wakes up, the first thing he does is make breakfast, and then he sits down to write a list, of things he wants to remember when he talks to Dorothy.

First, he wants an upfront cash settlement and a regular guaranteed income.

Second, he'll need help getting a work permit, maybe Playboy can help. They got hers in no time, but that'll be on her.

The final thing Paul is right on the list is, No divorce. She can have her legal separation, but there's no way he'll give Bogdonavich the satisfaction of marrying his wife.

Dorothy's meeting with her business manager is at 10.

He figures she'll be here no later than noon.

His roommate, Patti has plans to go roller skating, so she won't be here.

He tells her he'll meet her and a friend after he's done with Dorothy around 2:00 PM.

He doesn't want anyone in the house when Dorothy's here.

He and Mark Goldstein have agreed Goldstein will periodically check-in.

They talked about Paul wearing a wire, the plan was to get Dorothy on tape saying she'll take care of Paul or anything related to financial support, something they could use in a claim.

But then they couldn't find the gear or figure out how to put it together, but they had a new plan.

Goldstein says he'll be outside watching while Dorothea's here, following her when she leaves the check-in regularly by phone to make sure everything is OK.

He checks his watch at 9:30 AM, waits until 11, and then calls Robert Houston.

Dorothy will be there by then.

He reminds Houston he wants Dorothy to buy him a house.

He'll tell him to have Dorothy call before she leaves.

He wants to make sure before she arrives that everything is perfect.

At 10:30 AM, Dorothy arrives at Bob Houston's office.

He ushers her into the conference room, where he's got a stack of papers for her to sign and a box of cheques for her corporate account.

And then he hands over a form for a new American Express card.

It will be Dorothy's first, and she's excited.

I'm thinking about buying a car, she says shyly.

Her 1967 Cougar is falling apart, and Paul sold the Jaguar she got as part of her Playmate Prize package.

Let me lease one for you something nice, Houston says you can afford it.

Dorothy's smile fades, but what if I have to give all the money to Paul?

You won't, he says, don't worry so much. You're meeting with Marty Croft tomorrow for a lead in his film, if you get it, pays $100,000.

Houston's Secretary buzzes in to tell them Paul is on the phone; he wants to talk to Houston.

Let me take it in my office, he says.

When he comes back, he tells her Paul told him that Dorothy is going to his house this morning.

Dorothy suddenly feels guilty and said I know what you're thinking, but he's been nice about this whole thing, and I'd like to keep it that way.

Houston says she doesn't have to do that.

He says we're at the stage where the lawyers should be doing the talking about the division of property.

Dorothy tells Houston she appreciates his concern, but it's better this way.

Then she asked to use the phone to let Paul know she was heading over.

When she hangs up, she tells Houston, I'm hoping Paul and I can stay friends.

****

On Thursday, August 14th, Goldstein pulls up to the curb across the street from 1081 West Clarkson Rd, Paul's House.

He shuts off the engine and rolls down the window, Dorothy's already here for all the green cougars parked on the street.

He looks at his watch at 12:30 PM.

He picks up his Car phone and dials, Paul picks up right away, as if he's expecting him because he is.

Everything OK? Goldstein asks.

Paul tells him Dorothy's there and everything is fine.

Goldstein says he'll check in later, then hangs up the phone and waits, listening to the traffic on the 10 freeway.

He fiddles with the radio and tells his seat back.

THE MURDER OF A STARLET

Hard to know how long he'll be sitting here before Dorothy leaves.

Two hours later and she still hasn't come out, he picks up the phone and dials again, this time there is no answer, maybe they kissed and made up.

He looks at the time, it's 2:30 PM.

He'll give it a couple more hours and try again.

At 5:00 PM, Patty arrives back at the house with her friend Lynn.

She's not sure why Paul never showed up at the roller rink. She tried calling, but no one picked up.

Maybe he and Dorothy are still talking, her car is still here.

Inside, the two girls notice Paul's bedroom is Doors closed. Dorothy's purses on the living room floor, Patty shrugs.

Maybe they want to be left alone.

The girls sit down to watch the evening News, but it's hard to concentrate because Paul's phone keeps ringing but no one comes out of the bedroom to answer it.

A few minutes later it rings again.

Finally, Lynn says let's get something to eat I can't take this shit.

At 6:30 PM, Patty and Len exit the house, and Goldstein watches them drive away.

He still hasn't been able to reach Paul, but if something was wrong, the two women would have done something, So why is he picking up the phone?

At 7:30 PM, Steve Krishnan gets home.

Goldstein tries Paul again but no answer.

He wonders why no one gets the German shepherd out of the backyard, he's been barking for hours.

It's 8 pm Patty drop off at the house and almost completely dark now.

Goldstein can see the flicker of the TV bounce off the sliding glass doors of the upstairs balcony.

He keeps calling Paul, *what are they doing in there?* He thinks.

At 11:30 PM, Goldstein decides to do something he never does.

THE MURDER OF A STARLET

He punches in the number to Steve Kushner's private line upstairs.

Patty jumps when she hears Steve's phone, the constant ringing downstairs has her on edge.

I'll get it, she tells Steve.

It's Goldstein, he wants to talk to Steve.

Patty hands over the phone and watches Steve's face.

He sang, Sorry, I haven't seen him all day.

Then there's a pause and he sets down the phone.

He tells Patty he's going to check on Paul.

You wanna come? He asks.

Patty shakes her head suddenly she's afraid to go downstairs.

But after a couple of minutes, her curiosity wins out, she softly pads down after him.

When she gets to the bottom, she can see Steve standing in the doorway to Paul's Room.

She only catches a glimpse of what's inside, then Steve turns in, crashes into her, and says, " Jesus, don't go in there, he says, and runs up the stairs.

She doesn't, but she'll never forget what she saw in that split-second glimpse.

Inside his car, Goldstein hears a loud clattering and then Kushner's back.

They are dead, they're both dead, Goldstein feels sick.

911, what is your emergency?

Some bad as happened, at 10881 W Clarkson Road, two people died.

She repeated the address back to him, and he said yeah.

He hangs up the phone and looks at his watch, 12:15 AM, he takes a deep breath.

He needs to go inside when he calls Hugh Hefner to give him the news.

He is in the game room playing pinball with friends. When the call comes in, *this is Mark Goldstein*, the man, on the other hand, says *sorry to disturb you at this time of night, but I thought you ought to be the first to know, Paul and Dorothy are dead.*

At first, Hef thinks it's a prank, some cruel joke, it's not until Goldstein hands the phone to a police officer who has learned the unthinkable is true.

The policeman tells him they're still waiting for the investigating officer.

But yes, they're both dead.

Hef puts down the phone, his hands are shaking.

He looks around the room at the people he was laughing with just a few minutes ago.

Now the women are crying, the men stunned and shocked in disbelief.

Hefner turns away and picks up the phone, It's late, but it's a call he has to make before it's all over the news.

All day, Peter has had a nagging sick feeling in the pit of his gut, but he's not sure why.

It started when Dorothy didn't come home at 2:30 PM, it got worse at 6:00 PM and Dorothy's sister confessed her secret.

Dorothy told her she had to go see Paul.

Paul? He asks.

The first thing that raced through his mind was that he lost her, but he quickly shook it off.

At 7:00 PM, Peters's friend offered to drive him to Paul's house, but Peter didn't want to create more problems.

Since then, Peters has been on edge, he keeps looking at his watch.

Call Dorothy he says, and the phone rings at 12:30 AM he feels a pang of relief, there she is, he says.

But it's not Dorothy, it's Hefner.

His voice is soft. Peter, have you heard? Hefner asks.

Peter is confused, no he said, what are you talking about?

Oh God.

Now Peters's heart is pounding.

What's the matter Hef what's going on? Peter asks.

There's a pause, and then Hefner tells him Dorothy is dead.

It takes a moment for Peter to register what he heard.

When it does, he drops the phone and sinks to the floor, he stands up and takes 3 halting steps, then falls again. Cross up into a bar, and sobs.

The police arrived on the scene at 12:20 AM.

Dorothy's purses are in the middle of the living room.

Downstairs inside the room Dorothy and Paul once shared, they find two naked bodies covered in blood, their clothes strewn across the floor.

Dorothy lays across the corner of the low bed.

Her knees are on the floor in her face, turned down.

She almost looks like she's sleeping, except for the shotgun blast to the left side of her face.

The tip of her forefinger is missing as if she raised her hand to her face in self-defence.

There are bloody hand prints on her left leg, her buttocks, and her left arm and shoulder.

Paul's body is near the door, face down, his head shattered by a large powder-burned wound.

The Mossberg shotgun is under his body.

Strands of long blonde hair are clutched in his blood-covered hand. The police investigation concludes murder-suicide which is later confirmed by the coroner.

Dorothy died instantly, and Schneider took his own life about an hour later.

The report also notes near Stratten's head at an angle away from her is a loveseat sexual appliance on the floor.

It was set into a position for possible rear-entry intercourse.

In some of the news stories, the press will run with this detail, speculating Dorothy was violently sodomized.

But the autopsy report paints a different, more confusing picture.

THE MURDER OF A STARLET

A coroner's official tells a reporter that no injury to Dorothy was consistent with violent intercourse.

No contusions on her wrists or ankles to indicate force.

Swabs from her genitals show evidence of intercourse, but the tests could not say for certain when she last had sex.

They don't find a suicide note, but there are two personal letters near the scene.

One is on Paul's nightstand, a five-page letter from one of the girls Paul was dating.

In it, she calls Paul's obsession with Dorothy sick.

The second is a rambling letter from Paul to Dorothy, it was found in Dorothy's purse along with $1100 in cash.

In the letter, Paul complains about being broke and accuses her of abandoning him.

No one knows exactly what happened that afternoon except the two people involved, but the end is the same.

THE MURDER OF A STARLET

Dorothy Stratten's meteoric rise to stardom is cut short, two years and one day after her arrival in Hollywood.

She was just 20 years old.

****

Friday, August 15th Dorothy's death is front page news around the world.

Eight days after her murder, Dorothy's ashes are laid to rest at Westwood Village cemetery, not far from the grave of Marilyn Monroe.

Dorothy's family flies down from Vancouver for the funeral.

Peter and Hef attend, along with Garbowsky, Mario Cassilly, and Elizabeth Norris, three of the people Dorothy was close to from the Playboy family.

A pink granite headstone purchased by Peter Bogdonavich marks her grave.

The epitaph was chosen by him, a quote from a farewell to Arms, the Hemingway novel Dorothy was reading before she died.

THE MURDER OF A STARLET

Paul's body is sent back to Vancouver for burial, forever exiled from Hollywood.

His family files a claim against Dorothy's assets.

With the help of Playboy's lawyers, Nelly can get the legal action thrown out of court.

Dorothy's murder nearly destroys Peter Bogdonavich.

He throws himself into finishing his movie.

They all laughed as a tribute to her, but the studio refuses to release it, fearing the public won't want to see a comedy or one of its stars have been brutally murdered.

Against the advice of colleagues and friends, Bogdonavich mortgages his home to buy the film and distributed it himself.

It's a disaster he will later deeply regret.

It will take him years to recover financially.

In 1984, Peter published a book about Dorothy's life called, *The Killing of the Unicorn.*

He uses the book to go after his old friend Hugh Hefner, blaming the Playboy machine for her death.

The feud is ugly, personal, and very public.

A year later, when Hef has a stroke, he mentions it as a cause.

The falling out will last until after Hefner died in 2017 at 91, where he's laid to rest in the same cemetery as Dorothy.

In the mid-1980s, rumors circulate that Bogdonavich is in a relationship with Dorothy, sister Louise, Tall, blonde, and blue-eyed, the public sees her as an almost eerie doppelganger of Dorothy.

The two were married in 1988 and Louise eventually becomes Peters's producing partner.

When they divorced 12 years later, Bogdonavich continued to live with her, along with Nellie, Louise, and his mother.

They become an unusual but tight-knit family, bonded forever by their grief and their love for Dorothy.

Hefner will offer his tribute to Dorothy first with a nearly 100-page feature about her life, that he publishes in Playboy.

It's the longest ever written for the magazine.

Four years later, Playboy produced a glowing documentary, *Dorothy Stratten, The Untold Story*.

Toward the end of the documentary, Hef talks about the impact Dorothy had on everyone she met and how much she meant to him,

Dorothy was so special, so young, so beautiful, so full of life. That, it took me a very long time to get over it. And am not over it yet.

THE MURDER OF A STARLET

CONCLUSION

Dorothy Stratten's life was one of promise and potential, tragically cut short by the violence of a man who couldn't handle her success. She was more than just a blonde beauty or a Playboy centerfold; she was a young woman with dreams, talent, and a bright future ahead of her. Yet, beneath the glamour of Hollywood and fame, the dark side of obsession and control lurked in the shadows. Dorothy's story serves as a cautionary tale—a reminder of how fragile life can be and how fame often comes at a heavy price.

The starlet who had captivated so many was betrayed by the very people who claimed to love her. In the end, Dorothy's legacy is not defined by her murder but by the light she brought to those around her and the lasting impact she left on the world of film and pop culture. Her life and death have haunted Hollywood for decades, a tragic narrative that highlights the risks of the pursuit of fame in a world that can be as dangerous as it is alluring.

Dorothy Stratten's story will continue to resonate, reminding us of the humanity behind the headlines. She was a rising star whose light was extinguished far too soon, but her memory, and the lessons of her life, endure.

APPRECIATION

To all my readers, thank you from the bottom of my heart for joining me on this journey into the life and untimely death of Dorothy Stratten. I hope this story has not only captured your interest but also shed light on the complexities of fame, love, and the dangers that sometimes lurk behind closed doors.

Writing this true crime story has been a labor of love, and I couldn't have done it without your support, curiosity, and appreciation for the truth. Thank you for allowing me to share Dorothy's story with you. I hope you walk away with a deeper understanding of her life, her struggles, and the harsh realities of the world she found herself in.

Please stay tuned for future works, and thank you again for being a part of this journey.

With gratitude,

THE MURDER OF A STARLET

THE MURDER OF A STARLET

THE END

THE MURDER OF A STARLET

OTHER BOOKS WRITTEN BY THE AUTHOR

1. The killer among us: The Brutal killing of Bonne Lee Bakley (True crime series)
2. T R U E C R I M E S T O R I E S: Frightful True Crime Murder Cases For Your Late-Night True Crime Binge (True crime series)
3. The Tip of the Spear: A Sheriff Ryan Caldwell Story
4. The criminals from Texas: shocking true crime stories of murder, deception and assassination (True crime series)
5. The jersey shore thrill killer: A True crime serial killer compilation that will send shivers down your spine (True crime series)
6. The Case of the Disappearance Blonde : A shocking True crime (A Private Detective's Relentless Pursuit of Justice) (True crime series)

Printed in Dunstable, United Kingdom